My Brother's Things

Susan M. Szurek

Chapbook Press

Schuler Books
2660 28th Street SE
Grand Rapids, MI 49512
(616) 942-7330
www.schulerbooks.com

My Brother's Things

ISBN 13: 9781957169460

eBook ISBN 13: 9781957169491

Library of Congress Control Number: 2023910462

Printed in the United States by Chapbook Press.

Also by Susan M. Szurek:

Everstille: A Novel

Everstille's Librarian

Olivia from Everstille

Tomas' Children

Her Cousin Julia

Author's Note and Acknowledgement

It was a quiet warm summer night as Noreen, Mary Ellen, Joanne, Sharon, and I sat around the wonderfully carved century-old dining table in Sharon's home talking, eating, drinking, and laughing. At one point, Sharon opened a carefully designed coffer and showed us a beautifully jeweled chalice which belonged to her late brother, Father Bernard, who used it when celebrating Mass. It was now in her keeping, and she wondered aloud what should be done with the object she deemed holy. We admired the chalice, but none of us had any ideas. However, that instance was the impetus for this novel.

What do we, should we, do with personal effects left behind? Give them away? Sell them? Dispose of them? Perhaps, store them away for future generations to deal with? Those objects safeguard lore, contain history. Maybe even secrets. That night I came up with a tale about a priest and his chalice and outlined it to the others. But I did not write that story because it belongs to Father Bernard and Sharon.

I wrote this story.

This one is mine.

There is, after all, always something wonderful and touchingly beautiful about a young man, for the first time released from the bonds of schooling, making his first ventures toward the infinite horizon of the mind. At this point he has not yet seen any of his illusions dissipated, or doubted either his own capacity for endless dedication or the boundlessness of the world of thought.

Herman Hesse

I.

The Box

*No permanence is ours; we are a wave
That flows to fit whatever form it finds.*

The Box

Even though I expected the box to arrive, I was surprised, as I parked in the driveway after work, to see it resting on my front porch. It had been some time since Steve and I drove to Indiana to take care of my brother and arrange for his cremation. My brother is currently sitting on the upper shelf of my closet, waiting for me to do something permanent with him. I haven't decided what to do yet.

Steve and I traveled to South Bend during the last days of the summer break. A week later, when we returned, tasks awaited us. There was a hurried back-to-school shopping trip for the kids, my unfinished preparation for the new high school history class I was to teach in the fall, and my mother-in-law's insistence that her son finish the restoration of her dining room table and chairs he had promised to complete for her birthday. Our kitchen was only half painted, the old oven needed replacing, the tomatoes in the vegetable garden were overripe, and it all needed immediate attention. The kitchen is still unfinished. So, the box, when it arrived, was simply another task for me to undertake, and I was not ready for it.

I went into the house through the garage door, placed my purse and bookbag on the kitchen table, gave a brief thought as to what dinner would be, and opened the front door where the box was waiting. I glanced at the return address and saw it was from the hospital in Indiana. We were told that when my brother was admitted, his leather duffle bag was on the ambulance gurney with him, but it was removed. It was taken, labeled, and placed in a storage area. Due to the complications about the accident and his subsequent death, it was forgotten when we arrived. A week or so after returning home, I received a phone call from someone there and was told that as soon as possible the bag would be boxed and sent to me, and I promptly forgot about it. And here it was. On the front porch.

It wasn't heavy or even large, but it was awkward. I dragged it into the front hallway and stood up. I was not ready to delve into this mystery. I didn't know what items were in it, but I knew it would take more than a cursory glance, and I was not mentally prepared for it yet. The box needed to be put away. I didn't need either of my teenagers coming home from school and wanting to dig into it. It was none of their business, and I was not sure what I would find. I opened the front closet and looked for a space. Towards the back on the floor, there was a large basket containing winter boots. Pulling it out, I realized that they would need to be reorganized, removed, or replaced. Jim was a senior and his feet were large. He had grown in the last year and would never fit into the boots that were there. Kate wouldn't wear hers either, although I suspected it was more of a style rejection than a size issue. There were some other boots which were mine, and some I didn't recognize, and before winter the entire basket needed to be tended to. But not today.

As I pulled out the boots to create a space and shoved the box into it, I wondered if I should drag it upstairs to my closet and allow these things to rest with the owner. But time was getting away, and in another few minutes, the two teens would return and see this. I could hear them asking, "Is this for me/us?", "Can we open it?", "What's in it?" *No, no,* and *I don't know* would be the answers, and I wasn't prepared to deal with their curiosity. I knew I would need some time when I was able to be solitary, to open the box, to look through the duffle bag which I knew was inside, to view what remained of my brother's life, and while secluded in my room, to confront my brother's things.

II.

My
Brother

I do not wish to go out into the world with an insurance policy in my pocket guaranteeing my return in the event of a disappointment, like some cautious traveler who would be content with a brief glimpse of the world. On the contrary, I desire that there should be hazards, difficulties, and dangers to face; I am hungry for reality, for tasks and deeds, and also for privation and suffering.

My Brother

i.

My brother was ten when I was born, fifteen when I was five, and twenty when I was ten. I have stored memories of him: helping me learn to ride a bike, teaching me to play chess, teasing me when a boy I liked showed up at the house to sit on the porch with me. The gap in our ages meant we never completely knew each other, and by the time I was twelve, he was twenty-two, grown, and gone. He was the one person in my life, the only person, I never really knew.

When he left, I didn't know where he went. Our parents never spoke about him in front of me, although I would hear his name as they spoke to each other in the kitchen or front room, quickly curtailing their conversation when I appeared. Before he left, he and Dad would argue. They would move through the yard and end up by the back fence, away from the house, talking with voices which became increasingly louder. During these times, Mom would be in the kitchen, pretending to complete tasks while watching the two of them through the kitchen window. Sometimes their discussions were short, fifteen minutes or so, but often they went on for over an hour, and as their voices became more strident, Mom would walk out to the back porch and stand there, then move down to the grass and quietly take another step closer, threatening them with her presence, with her sixty-two inches of motherliness and accelerating worry. Once they noticed her stealthy approach, they would stop the conversation, and Dad would walk into the house, past Mom, past me, into the front room where he would turn on the television and stare at it for the next hour. My brother would disappear. Sometimes he would be gone for an hour or two. Other times, for a day or two. I never knew what their arguments were about. I was young and didn't realize then the consequences of passionate discourse.

After high school, my brother attended a nearby college, living there, sharing an apartment with other students. He worked part-time, and during academic breaks, would come home to share our family dinners although he rarely stayed more than a couple days. Much of that time he would be in his room playing the drum set that was shoved into the corner or plunking his guitar. He and Dad tried, for Mom's sake, to get along, but those times, those dinners, were filled with spiky edges. After some years of half-hearted education, his roommates left or graduated, and he came home for a week, piling some ragged furniture, the old guitar, and bags of kitchenware in the corner of the garage. He would sit in the yard, or poke around the hood of his old car, and when he wasn't doing that, he stayed in his room making lengthy phone calls to people I didn't know. I heard him talk to Jack or Tommy or Bud, but those were not the names of his previous roommates, and I didn't know any of his friends. Mom tried to talk to him about his future, about his plans and possible jobs, and asked about his current girlfriend, but he just said they had broken up, and he didn't know what he was going to do. Dad would come home from work, look at my brother, shake his head, and they would often engage in one of their talks which led to an uncomfortable evening for all of us.

Eventually, my brother disappeared. I should have realized he was going somewhere. He began to sell his things. Some teenagers came to the house, and he helped them carry his drum set to their car. Then the old furniture from the garage disappeared, and his guitar was gone. One day he got into his car, left, and came back on a motorcycle which he worked on for a few days. On my twelfth birthday, after dinner and birthday songs and cake, my brother gave me a bracelet which just fit on my wrist and which I still have. He kissed my head and whispered, "To remember me," and the following morning as the birthday balloons which had decorated the dining room wall for my celebration were found on the floor, the air easing out of them, the motorcycle was gone. So was my brother. He left a note. In his loopy handwriting he wrote:

Don't worry about me. I'll be fine. I'll stay in touch.

Underneath the pithy note was scrawled a large artistic *J*. That was his signature.

Jonathan.

Jab.

***

ii.

Jonathan Alexander Boyd. Jab.

Alexander was my father's name and his father's name, and Dad insisted upon bestowing the name to his firstborn, his only son. But Mom wanted *Jonathan* for his name, and, according to the story Jab told me once, this was the only time Mom got her way. "A *Jab* is what I am, and that's why they call me that. Dad didn't want to call me by my first name because that would be admitting defeat," and my brother laughed and pulled my ponytail. "Lucky you weren't named *Sally Lou Oona*", and I giggled when I realized the possibility of being called *Slob*. I was Janet Oona Boyd, and happy to be called *Jan* and not *Job* although the strange middle name, an ancestral moniker, was weird enough, and I only confided it to my best friend once I thought I could trust her.

I adored Jab. He was funny, and when he did pay attention to me, it was as though we were in another world. He would repeat strange things to me, and I didn't understand most of them. When I would ask him what it meant he would say, "Think about it, baby sister," and just smile. *No permanence is ours; we are a wave that flows to fit whatever form it finds* was one of his favorite sayings and so, I remember it. He had written on a large sheet of paper *Truth is lived, not taught,* and taped it above his bed. It stayed there through his college years. When he left, it remained: faded, and ragged at the corners, the tape yellowing and tearing, and I wondered why my parents allowed it to stay crookedly dangling from the wall in his room. Later, I understood it as a talisman, a protector of sorts. Keeping it there would keep my brother safe.

He returned for a while when I was almost fifteen, riding a different motorcycle that was smoky and noisy. He parked it at the side of the house and arrived just as we were sitting down to dinner. When he appeared at the back door, he hugged Mom and me, and then went to Dad. They hugged for a long time and spoke although I couldn't hear the words. Jab brought in his leather duffel bag which turned out to be filled with dirty clothes. After we ate, Mom asked for the clothes. He gave them to her, and she took them to the laundry room while he went upstairs to take a long shower. He yelled *good-night* to us and went to bed right away. It was almost noon the following day when he woke up and came downstairs for coffee. As he drank it, I examined him, thinking he looked older than his years. I supposed the beard and long hair which was pulled back into a ponytail had something to do with it. It seemed to me that during the time he spent with us both he and Dad were trying not to argue. Jab was on his best behavior. They managed to get along most of the week he stayed.

But twice they were at the back fence, and the discussion got loud, and as Mom began her feline, noiseless stalking of them, they noticed and quieted down, and came back into the house together.

I was thrilled to see my brother and spent as much time with him as I could. School had just ended for the year, and I would be a junior in the fall, but because I was still too young to get a summer job, I hung around him during the few days he stayed. I talked constantly. I asked him a million questions. I wanted to know where he had been, and what he had done, and who were his friends. More than a couple times I questioned him about the possibility of staying at home with his family. Why did he have to leave? Why did he need to travel? Why couldn't he remain with me? He would laugh and shake his head and say, "Still my baby sister," and never answered most of my queries.

"I've been around, Jan, been looking at the world and wondering. That's how to learn about it all. No, I don't have a single girlfriend, but have many friends of many kinds," and when I asked what he meant by that, to explain it to me, he laughed again and quoted, "*And life may summon us to newer races*," then reached out and pulled my ponytail and smiled.

"Can I ride on your motorcycle?' I asked as he continued to tinker with it at the side of the house. He said it needed work and didn't want to take a chance with me on the back but had to adjust some things. I would stand and watch him working with Dad's tools, changing this and tightening that. One morning, we walked together to an automotive store where he purchased additional parts for it. As we walked back to the house, he spoke to me, and his tone was serious.

"Listen, Jan, I'm going to give you a phone number, but you are not to call it unless there is an emergency, a *real* emergency. The number belongs to a friend named Mark, and if you really, really need to get in touch with me, tell him what you need, and I'll get the message. You're old enough to do that, and to understand that this is important. Mom and Dad don't need to know about this, and I'm trusting you with this information because I believe I can. Understand?"

"Sure," I answered, "I promise, Jab," and felt older than my almost fifteen years. He trusted me. I figured he was going to fix his motorcycle and leave in the next day or two. Gone again. The last time I saw him, he gave me a bracelet and disappeared. He was giving me something again. Two days later, when I woke up, his duffel bag containing his clean clothes was not there. Neither was the motorcycle, and I knew he would not return. I kept the phone number hidden, but looked at it so often, I memorized it. I wondered what would constitute a "real emergency"? I considered reasons which would be important enough to use the number, to act on this gift, but nothing came to mind.

***

iii.

During the summer after my senior year, when I was working at a local restaurant waiting tables and making plans to start college in the fall, I had a reason to use the number Jab had given me. Our father had a heart attack and died, and I assumed this was enough of a real emergency. I called the number three times. No one answered the first two times even though I let it ring a dozen times before giving up. I would have left a message had there been a machine, but there wasn't. The third time it rang four times, and the male voice that breathlessly answered said, "What?"

"This is Janet Boyd, Jonathan's, Jab's sister. He gave me this phone number to get in touch with him if I needed to. Is this Mark?"

"Yeah. I'm Mark. What's the problem?"

"I need to get in touch with Jab. Our father died, and he needs to know. Can I talk to him, please?"

There was a long silence before Mark spoke. "Sorry to hear that, but Jab's not around. I can get the message to him though. Is there anything else you want to tell him?"

I was so saddened I could barely speak. I was sure I would be able to speak to Jab and didn't expect I would not be able to. I needed to hear his voice, to share my sorrow, but this was the best I could do. I swallowed my tears and said, "The wake is in two days and the funeral is the following day. Please tell Jab. Please tell him to come home as soon as possible. If he can call, that would be great."

"I'll let him know as soon as I can. Again, sorry about this. Sorry about your father. Listen, I have to go. Don't worry; I'll let your brother know," and the phone call ended.

I held the phone, listening to the silence, and thought I should call back, but there was nothing else to say. I cried for a time, then wiped my eyes and went downstairs to the kitchen where Mom and some of the neighbors were gathered. They had come over bearing casseroles and cakes and were talking to and consoling Mom. I was unsure whether I should tell her I had tried to call Jab. I didn't want her to realize I had known a way to contact him and never told her, so I thought it was best to say nothing. I couldn't add to her sorrows if Jab didn't show up.

He didn't. At least not for the wake or the funeral. I was angry and upset and nervous, thinking that every loud sound I heard was his motorcycle and felt frustrated when it was not. Mom and I got through that awful time somehow. I tried to soothe her the best I could, but I remained bitter and outraged that my brother had not shown up or even called. No matter what I did, I couldn't comfort Mom when she cried because she missed the two men in her life. So did I.

After the funeral and the luncheon, after telling relatives and friends good-bye, after coming home to a muted house, we were exhausted. Mom and I went to our rooms and to bed early that night. I had the next few days off from work, and we planned to sort through Dad's things and reorganize our lives without him. It was still light when I crawled under my covers and fell into an exhausted sleep. I was awakened early the next morning when I heard a motorcycle drive up alongside the house. When I went to my side bedroom window and peered out, there was Jab, taking off his helmet, holding his duffel bag, and walking around to the back of the house. I ran down the steps and flung open the screen door just as he reached for its handle. I stood there, tears running down my face and wasn't sure which I would do first: hug him or hit him.

He dropped his bag and hugged me, and we both wiped away tears. "So sorry, Jan, I couldn't get here before this. I tried, but I was far away. Are you OK? Is Mom OK?"

I shook my head. "No, Jab, we're not OK. We're awful. Dad is gone, and you weren't here, and Mom is a mess, and I'm supposed to start college in a month, and I missed you and…" I couldn't continue. Tears overwhelmed me.

Jab led me to a kitchen chair and sat me down. He looked around the kitchen for the box of tissue Mom kept there and placed in front of me. I grabbed a handful to wipe my eyes and blow my nose while Jab went to the drawer where the clean kitchen towels were and wet one at the sink. He brought it to me and held it on the back of my neck before giving it to me so I could place it against my face. He waited for me to calm down. Finally, I did. When I looked at him, Jab was wiping his tears with the back of his hand, and then it was my turn to wipe his face. We sat down at the kitchen table where Jab reached over and held my hands. We were silent. Finally, I got up and went to the counter and started a pot of coffee. As it brewed, I sat down again. We looked at each other.

"I'm sorry, Jan. Things have been strange. Mark did get in touch with me. He tried for two days, and when I got the message, I left to get here. I'm sorry I wasn't in time, but I'll stay for a while now, and help if I can. I feel so awful about this."

The tears came down his face and he put his hands over it and sat crying for a time. I pushed the tissue box over to him and got up to pour us both some coffee. I opened the fridge, taking out the milk, and fixed his coffee the way he liked it. He wiped his face, tried to give me a smile, and we sipped at the coffee as we spoke. He wanted to know about Dad and what happened and the wake and funeral and where Dad was buried and I told him everything I could. We were still there an hour later when Mom came downstairs. When she saw Jab sitting there, she started to cry, and it seemed to me that for the next few days, whenever we were together, one of us would begin to cry. I guess that's what death does.

Jab stayed through the rest of the summer and into the fall as I started college. Mom went back to work after some time, and for a while, the three of us fell into a routine. Jab cleaned the house, took care of the yardwork, and cooked for us. He had picked up some culinary skills and was serving us tasty meals, things we had never tried before: pasta primavera, Asian stir-fries, quiche. We liked them all. After dinner, the three of us would sit and talk about our days, and Jab offered advice about college. He told me that he may not have finished, but I needed to and encouraged me to be diligent. Mom told stories about Jab when he was young and how she worried about him because he never stayed in one place, even as a toddler. "From his start, Jab had a wandering soul," Mom said and we laughed. We spoke about Dad, and I learned things that happened the years before I was born. I was glad Jab and Mom were able to laugh and reminisce about those first ten years before I came along. Those years when Dad was still here.

We were content together. Jab helped us get through that difficult time of grieving by just being with us. Time passed, and I started my college classes. I was a commuter student because I didn't want Mom to be alone, and I would get up early each morning to prepare for the day. One day, in early fall, I woke up to the sound of Jab's motorcycle whirling into life and traveling quickly down the street. As it faded into the distance, I realized I expected this. Two days earlier, when I came home from classes, I found Jab doing laundry, making sure his clothes were clean and folded. After that night's dinner (pineapple chicken), right before I went upstairs to bed, Jab handed me a book. It was obviously not new and had been thoroughly read. It was called *Siddhartha,* and I frowned when he handed it to me.

"So, you're assigning me reading now? What are you? A wise old teacher?" and I glanced through the book.

Jab smiled. "Nope, not me. The book explains about someone who was though. Give it a read, Jan. You might like it," and he hugged me good-night. He was gone soon after that. He left us a note which read:

Love you both. Time for me to get going, but don't worry about me. I'll be in touch. J.

Mom cried for a while. It seemed the tears would never stop, but eventually, the two of us adjusted to just the two of us. Later that day, the day Jab left again, I went up to his room to gather the sheets from his bed. There was another note meant for me which he left on his pillow. It said:

Little Sister,
I'm proud of you. You are strong and capable. I am leaving because I want to <u>find</u>. "Seeking means: having a goal. But finding means: being free, being open, having no goal." (from the book I gave you). Remember Mark's number?

Love you. J.

***

iv.

During the next few years, we would sometimes hear from Jab. A few postcards arrived, a short message in his loopy handwriting telling us he was in Missouri or traveling through Texas or visiting another state. Rarer were the phone calls. They were always brief, and he generally sounded breathless and in a hurry. He told us he was traveling around the country, making friends, working at all sorts of jobs, learning about life, and that we shouldn't worry about him. He was happy and missed us, and yes, he would be home sometime for a visit, but no, he couldn't give us a current address. He was traveling through, or staying with friends, or needed to get to his job, or to meet someone, or something similar. Mom and I discussed these messages and calls, tearing apart the words, searching behind the short sentences for hidden meanings or significant notions, but never coming up with anything of consequence. We took what we could from his meager correspondences and conversations, eased our heartstrings, and waited for the next message while we continued being and living.

We managed to pull together and organize our lives without either Dad or Jab. There were times which were difficult, especially around the holidays and the anniversary of Dad's passing, but we kept busy. Mom went back to work full-time, and I was busy with my job and school. We shared the chores around the house and hired a neighbor boy who was willing to mow the grass and shovel the snow during appropriate seasons, so we didn't need to worry about those two time-consuming tasks.

I had discovered a joy in reading and researching about history and decided that I wanted to be a teacher. Because I was so busy either working or studying, I didn't have much of a social life. I had friends, but living at home and commuting to school took much of my leisure time. But when I met Steven Henderson during my senior year, I liked him enough to make time for him. We dated, learned about each other, stayed together, and married during my second year of teaching. We were both twenty-three, and I was certain that during the small family wedding to be held during the summer break, I would have Jab beside me, walking me down the aisle. I still had Mark's phone number and dialed it. This time, he answered the phone the first time it rang.

"Hello, Mark? This is Jab's sister, Jan. I need to get in touch with him. Is he there?"

"Nope. Sorry. Jab's not around. What can I do for you?"

"Can you get in touch with him and tell him I'd like to speak to him? We haven't heard from him for months, and I want him to know I'm getting married and wish he would come home for the wedding."

There was silence before Mark spoke. It made me nervous.

"Sure, I can get in touch with him, but it might take a week or so. I'll let him know. Congrats!"

"Thanks, Mark. Please tell him to call as soon as he can. The wedding is in about a month."

"Will do," and that was the end of the call.

I waited. Every day after school, I hurried home to check the mail, but no postcards came. No phone calls either. I thought about calling Mark again, but wasn't sure I should. This wasn't a real emergency. I just wanted Jab home. I wanted him to walk me down the church aisle. I wanted him to meet Steve, and I wanted to talk to him about his life and mine. The time passed, and there was no communication. I called Mark again, but there was no answer any of the three additional times I dialed his number. Between regular chores and jobs and planning for the wedding, I didn't have much time to brood about my brother's absence. I still held hope that I would hear from him, but I didn't. Jab never called, and Mom and Steve's father held my arms as I walked down the short path to the front of the church. The tears I cried were not all happy.

Steve and I settled into a small rented apartment and worked to save our money for a house. We both took on part-time jobs in addition to our regular ones, and the unfortunate upshot of that was I didn't spend as much time with Mom as I wanted to. One day, a rare day I wasn't working both jobs, Mom called when she got home from work.

"Jan, a package was delivered here for you. I think it's from Jab although there's no return address, but the postmark is from New Mexico. Why don't you come over to get it, and stay for dinner? Is Steve working tonight? He should come too."

"Steve is working, but give me an hour to do a few things around here and I'll be over. Don't fuss for dinner. In fact, I'll stop and pick something up for us," and with that plan in place, we hung up. I did a quick cleaning of the apartment and threw some clothes in a basket to take to Mom's. I would wash and dry them there while we ate and talked.

The package was waiting on the kitchen table when I walked it. It held three items: two hand-made baskets and a brief letter from Jab. The smaller basket was meant for Mom, and the larger one was for me. According to the note that came with them, these were woven baskets made by one of the artists from the Jicarilla Apache tribe in New Mexico. The baskets were amazing. Their sides and bottoms were woven with geometric patterns: squares and triangles and lines, and the brown, yellow, and red colors were bright. But it was the letter we read and reread which was the best gift. Jab apologized for not making the wedding. His motorcycle was unrepairable at the time, and he was working at some restaurant and doing other side jobs, and saving money for a truck, so he couldn't travel home. He was well and enjoyed his life, and wished my husband and me the best of everything. I realized he didn't even know Steve's name, and that realization made me choke up. The letter was brief…too brief…as all his messages were, and we didn't learn much more about him or his life than before the package was opened. We held the baskets, examining the workmanship and talked about them and Jab.

"Do you think he's living with the tribe?" asked Mom.

I looked at her and shrugged. "Mom, I know just as much as you do. There's no return address or phone number, and until Jab gets in touch again, we can only guess at what's going on."

We spent the evening admiring the baskets, deciding where we would display them, and wondering out loud about Jab. Mom told me to take the letter home and share it with Steve which I did. I still have it. I still have my basket too. It's on the hallway table. When I pass by it, I often reach out and touch it. And when, some years later, Mom died, I took her basket to my home and found a way to hang it on the wall in the hallway above mine.

Two woven siblings.

*****

v.

I called Mark one more time. Mom hadn't been feeling well, and I took her to the doctor who immediately put her in the hospital for tests. Stage four. She lasted barely two months, and the same day we found out the test results, I called Mark. There was no answer because the phone number had been disconnected. Despite that, I tried again, daily for a week, but finally gave up. I was devastated. And angry. What was wrong with my brother? Why couldn't he just call weekly? Or send an address? Or come home and stay and live a regular life? Why did he feel the need to wander? Couldn't he settle down in one place? Steve, who had never met Jab tried to stick up for him, and we fought about the brother-in-law he didn't know and had never met. Those were awful months. And then there was the house.

Everything came to me. The house, all its furnishings and papers, the fence which was falling at the back gate, Mom's clothes and personal effects, her car which she had neglected and had to be towed to the shop. It was all mine, and I had to deal with it. The house needed to be emptied and cleaned and sold, and that took forever. We held some garage sales and got rid of most of the furniture, household items, and clothes. I went through the rest of the things, and saved some items for myself. Photographs, important papers, and some memorabilia were put into a large plastic box and stored in the basement of our new house until I felt I had the fortitude to go through it all. Useful clothing, furniture, kitchen ware, knick-knacks were given away to thrift shops with the wish they would find a second life, and the garbage cans in the alleyway were filled and emptied and filled again. But the last thing I did, the final cleaning I had to face was Jab's room. I considered just letting Steve do what he offered to do: go in and empty it all and clean it. He said he could throw it all away and not care because he had no connection to the owner, but I just couldn't allow that to happen. The room had been left alone. Mom had kept it pretty much as it was when Jab left, hoping he would return for a visit, but it wanted cleaning and organizing. There were times I suggested that I could clean it out and make decisions about the books and papers which were there, but Mom always refused the offer. She said that it needed to be left for Jab. For him to return and take what he wanted or perhaps, to live in it again. I couldn't upset her, so I stopped asking and left the room as it was. Mom regularly went in and dusted and cleaned and made sure it was ready for the son who never returned. And then, out of some form of protection or guardianship or obligation, the dealing with it fell to me.

I waited until my spring break, and on the Monday of that week, when Steve went to work, I left to go to Mom's house and deal with the room. It was the last thing to be cleaned out before we put the house up for sale, and Steve had dragged boxes and bags and cleaning equipment there for my use. He told me he would be over after work and said I should wait for him to help, but I needed to get started. I parked in the driveway, opened the door to my childhood home, and walked in.

The house was empty except for the occasional stray rag or forgotten item, and I went through all the rooms before going upstairs. I stopped at the kitchen window and looked out to the back fence where I could envision the ghosts of Dad and Jab standing. I remembered how Mom would creep down the back patio steps thinking she could corral them, round them up like two snorting bulls, bring them back as friends. I stood for a time, then went to the patio door to check that it was locked and went up the stairs.

I peeked into the two empty bedrooms and then went to Jab's room which remained filled with his books and papers. I wasn't sure where to begin, so I opened the window and allowed the clean spring breeze to wander through the curtains. I examined what was in his closet and thought there was little that needed saving. There were some clothes I recognized from his high school and college days, some worn out shoes, and miscellaneous items. I sorted them into two piles: garbage and thrift store, but most went into the garbage. I began to take down the posters and the hand-printed sign over his bed and wondered if I should start a third pile: keep for Jab. But the posters and sign were old and torn and ripped, and I was still angry at Jab's disappearing act, so they went into the garbage. I thought I didn't want to spend more than one day doing this. We had the realtor coming on Thursday. Steve and a friend of ours would move out the furniture as soon as I was done, and I hurried my actions.

I went through the desk quickly, assuming anything Jab thought was important he would have taken with him. I got sidelined for a while looking through some pencil sketches of weird creatures he had drawn. It looked like he had started to create a comic book, but if he didn't take them, I wasn't going to keep them either. Garbage. There were several books, and I saved the ones which were in good shape. Thrift store. As I was moving a large pile of them into a box, a book with a blue cover fell on the floor, and I bent to pick it up. Inside the cover, in Jab's florid handwriting was printed:

*No permanence is ours; we are a wave
That flows to fit whatever form it finds.*

I recognized one of Jab's favorite sayings. I turned the book around to look at the title. It was *The Glass Bead Game* by Herman Hesse, and as I flipped through the pages, I noted the underlinings and circles and comments made by Jab, and decided that this was one item I would keep. I put it outside the door, close to the staircase so I would not forget it, and continued the cleaning.

I completed the cleaning of Jab's room that day, and when Steve came after work, I was sitting on the back patio steps holding the book, the only thing I had saved from his room. He looked at me, bent down to kiss me and asked, "Finished? That was faster than I thought. Tomorrow, Hugh and I will move the furniture out. Is everything sorted? What do you want to keep?"

"Just this," and I held up the book. "That's all. I dragged the garbage bags out, and the boxes upstairs will go to the thrift store. I think we're done here. I'll go home and call the cleaning company and arrange for them to come. They told me that they only needed one day's notice, so they can get here quickly. I'll also call some local thrift stores and find out about when and where to drop off the boxes. Let's lock up and go home. I want to take a shower, and would you mind leftovers tonight?"

"Sure. That's fine. Let's go. I'll call Hugh when we get home, and we'll get the furniture tomorrow. Going to read that?"

I glanced at the book in my hand. I never read the other book Jab gave me, and doubted I would read this one, but I said, "Maybe. I don't know. Certainly not tonight anyway, but I want to keep it. I'm ready. Let me get my purse and lock up. Meet you at home."

We got into our separate cars and drove home. I took the book with the blue cover and put it into my bottom dresser drawer next to some woolen socks and a winter hat. I thought I would look at it later, would examine the sentences Jab underlined and read his comments. But not tonight. Not now. Now I needed to shower and put on clean clothes and complete the necessary phone calls. I was tired and sad and didn't want to think any more about Jab or Mom or the house. I just wanted to sit on our new couch in our new house and pretend everything was fine. That's what I did.

***

vi.

When our son, James Henderson, was born, I considered giving him the middle name of *Jonathan*, and then thought about keeping the family name *Alexander*, but it was Steve who suggested *Jab* as a possibility. I hesitated at first because it had been a long time since we had heard from my brother. A while after both Mom and the house were gone, we received a forwarded postcard sent from Wyoming. He had sent it to the old house, and I realized he didn't even know his mother had died or that he now had a nephew who was almost eighteen months old. That postcard was the last we heard from Jab. There was nothing of importance on the card; just the usual comment about he's well and busy and traveling. I allowed James' middle name to become *Jab*, but hoped it would not portend his future; that he would not take after his wandering uncle. His absent uncle. My brother who I hadn't seen in years. At least not until the day he showed up on our front porch.

I took a maternity leave for the first year of Jim's life. Before the new school year began, Steve and I discussed our finances, and I knew I needed to go back to work. We found a reliable woman, Loretta Hanson, to care for Jim. It turned out to be a good match for us, so I returned to teaching. After school, I'd stop at Loretta's house and pick Jim up and go home where I would play with him before starting dinner. After dinner and dishes, when the weather was good, Steve and I would walk Jim around a block or two, pushing his stroller when he was a baby and following him on his little toddler push-car once he was older, then returning to complete the nightly routine and settle him in bed. In the evenings, we worked at our tasks: Steve preparing reports, me grading papers. On weekends we would labor at the house, painting and making improvements, or visit with friends and Steve's family, or take a weekend trip to a flea market or a museum. It was the usual suburban life, and we were happy.

It was a warm, late spring day, and I was wishing I hadn't assigned the papers I was lugging home to grade. Jim was in his car seat, blabbering away in his new little voice, singing songs, and making up words. As I turned the corner, I saw an unfamiliar truck parked in front of our house and wondered about it. I didn't see Jab sitting on the front steps until I pulled into the driveway and opened the door to step out. When he stood up and began to walk towards me, I froze. It had been years since I had seen him, but he looked the same. He also looked different. He was thinner and his hair was long and shaggy and pulled back into a messy ponytail. There was an old baseball cap on his head, and his beard was unkempt and scruffy. There was nothing that seemed particularly clean about him, and had it not been for his eyes and smile, I believe I would have passed him on the street and, casually, pulled my purse closer to me.

"Little sister!" he called, and he stood smiling at me.

I left Jim in the backseat, temporarily forgetting I had a child, and walked into Jab's arms. The anger and hurt I felt over the years left as we hugged, and I began to cry. He held me and didn't try to stop me, and it was only when I realized my son was crying at the same pitch as I was, that I remembered I had one. I pulled back and wiped my eyes and said, "Let me get Jim out of the back," and went to the car to remove my crying child.

I held Jim in my arms, and he stopped his crying but hid his face into my neck at the sight of the stranger who stood there. We stood for a minute talking, and then Jab laughed, and at that sound, Jim looked up and peeked around at his uncle.

"Well, look at this! What other surprises are there? If I had known about this one, I would have brought him something special from South Dakota," and Jab looked at me. "That's where I'm coming from. Been a long trip, Jan, and I'm glad to see you. Is there anything else I can bring in for you?"

He went to the car and grabbed my purse and bag from the front seat, and we walked together into the house. Once we got in, I took him to the kitchen where I put Jim on the floor with some toys and went to the fridge to pour us glasses of cold water. He asked for the bathroom, and when he went there, I started coffee and looked around for something to serve with it. But when he came back, he said, "Don't fuss. Let's talk," and we sat down.

"Jab, about Mom," I began.

"I know. I went to the house and saw the changes and talked to the neighbors. I know she's gone. That's how I found out your address. I didn't know about that one," and he nodded towards Jim who was busy building a tower, "and I wish I had."

"Jab, I don't want to fight. I haven't seen you in years and there have been many changes, but whose fault is it that you didn't know? I tried calling Mark, but the phone was disconnected, and I had no way of getting in touch with you."

He sat still and listened to me. There was a rueful expression on his face, and I thought he might cry, but he just sighed and looked at me.

"I know, Jan. I've lived the way I wanted to, and I realize not everyone understands. Maybe no one does. There are times I wonder about it myself. It's my fault, and I know that and accept it. There are so many things that have happened, and I can't even begin to talk about them. I'm sorry for not being here for Mom or for your wedding or for all the things I know I've missed. I have no excuses and won't make up any. All I can say is that I am here now and would like to stay for a while if you would have me. If not, I really do understand and can go. I won't stay long, I promise."

I looked at him and surprising both of us, I gave a laugh. "Of course you can stay here and stay as long as you want to. If there's one thing I know, it's that you probably won't stay long!"

We continued talking. We spoke about Mom and the old house, about my graduation and my teaching history at the high school. I grabbed the wedding album from a bookcase, and he looked at the photos. I talked about Steve and how we met. I showed him around the house and explained the plans we had for it. I tried to engage him and asked questions about his life but received vague, perfunctory answers. I backed off from pushing him for details. He was like a skittish animal, and I didn't want to scare him off. When Jim came over to me and leaned against my knee and watched this stranger talk and laugh, he grew curious, and at the point that Jab looked at his nephew and spoke to him, Jim walked over to him and held up his arms. Jab picked up my son and laughed as the child pulled on his beard and played with the hair that was absent from his own father's face. Eventually Jab went out to his truck and got his duffle bag, and I showed him to the guest room and bathroom, and left him to shower and work on his beard. I took Jim downstairs with me and settled him in his highchair while I gave him his dinner and began to prepare ours.

Jab stayed for almost three weeks. Steve and I continued our routine, and when we left for work each morning, Jab remained asleep. The second day he was there, Steve came home early, and I left the baby with his father as my brother and I took off. The first place we visited was the cemetery where our parents were buried. It closed at five in the evening, and the two of us stayed until that time, until the caretaker who was locking up came to us and kindly suggested it was time we leave. Then we went to the grocery store and shopped, and when it came time to pay, I pulled out my wallet, but Jab shook his head and said, "Put it away. This is the least I can do," and when he reached into his pocket and pulled out the biggest wad of cash I had ever seen, I let out a small shocked squeak which made Jab laugh.

"Sometimes I'm good at saving my pay. And sometimes, I'm lucky at cards," was all he said, and he paid for the many bags of groceries which we piled into the car and took home. Jab cooked for us that night and the rest of the nights he stayed with us. His culinary skills were impressive, and Steve and I enjoyed the meals he prepared for us. He did other things about the house during the time we were at work. The lawnmower was not working properly, and Jab tuned it up; then he cut the grass and weeded the garden, replacing the brown, dead shrubs with new ones he purchased. He fixed my washer because when he washed his dirty clothes, it made such a weird noise he knew something was wrong, so he examined the machine, bought the needed part, and repaired it. One day I came home and he was in the garage reorganizing the tools and placing them in a pegboard which he had bought and installed over Steve's workbench. He worked on his truck too, repairing and replacing what he needed to, making it ready for another trip. The meals were made, the house was cleaned, and items which were broken were repaired. I joked that if he wanted to stay, we would hire him as our chef and handy-man. The three of us walked around the block with Jim on his push car, and when I took him out of his car seat each afternoon, Jab was waiting there, and Jim couldn't wait to leave my arms and run into his. The weeks passed, and I was happy with Jab there, but I knew his wanderlust would return. It did.

The night before he left, I went to my bedroom and took out the blue-covered book, *The Glass Bead Game,* and brought it downstairs. I handed it to Jab and sat down beside him on the patio. He grinned when he saw it and thumbed through the pages. He stopped and read some of his remarks, the ones I never got around to reading. He looked at me.

"Did you read this book?"

I shook my head and sighed. "No, but I've been fairly busy. There has been little time for pleasure reading. I thought I would get around to it, but… It's the only thing I saved from your room. Don't know why, but I thought that if I saw you, you might want it back. It's yours."

Jab nodded and continued to look through the book. "Thanks, Jan. This was an important reason I've lived the way I have. It revealed ideas to me about humanity and education and philosophy. It gives a suggestion as to how all human knowledge can be linked, and I've found it enlightening. It encourages my understanding of life; it supports my wandering ways. I'd like to take it with me, if I can. Unless you want to keep it and read it."

"It's yours. Take it, Jab. I am so far behind in grading papers and doing other things, I just don't have time. I know what it is, and if I get a chance to do some reading, I'll pick a copy up."

We sat and watched the night around us, and when Steve came outside after putting Jim to bed, the three of us sat and talked about nothing of importance. Soon, Steve excused himself to finish some work. Jab and I were quiet for a while, but something warned me that this would be our last night together. I reached over and took his hand and held it as I said that to him.

He squeezed my hand. "I'm leaving tomorrow, Jan. I have treasured this time and want you to know that, but I've been here too long. I'll leave in the morning."

"Where are you going?"

"Not sure. I might head out west again. I might meet an old friend in Tennessee, but it will take some time to get there. Will make some stops along the way. Or maybe I'll go straight east. Not sure exactly. Listen, I'll try and do a better job of staying in touch this time. If I plop myself down somewhere for a while, I'll let you know, but I don't stay long in one place. OK?"

And there was nothing else for me to say except, "OK, Jab."

When the alarm rang the next morning, I got up and began to get ready for the day. Steve had gotten up earlier; I heard him downstairs. I went into the nursery to get Jim who was playing in his bed, and as I passed the guest room, the door was open and the room was empty. Jab hadn't waited until I was awake to leave. He was gone. I should have known that. I cleaned and dressed the baby, and we went downstairs where Steve was fixing breakfast and making coffee.

He looked at me and said, "He's gone. Look at this," and Steve held out a beaded keychain for me to admire. "Jab said he was given this as a gift when he went to some Indian ceremony. He was told to keep it until he found a worthy friend and then share it with him. Pretty nice, isn't it? I asked him to wait until you were up and offered him breakfast, but he said he needed to go, that the two of you spoke last night. There's something for you too. He left it on the hallway table in the basket," and he took Jim and placed him in his chair and gave him breakfast while I walked to the hallway.

There was a small brown bag tucked into the basket he had sent. I reached into it and took out a piece of paper into which something had been wrapped. Into my hands fell a silver chain, and on the chain was a tiny perfectly designed silver dragonfly. Before I read the letter, I took the necklace and hung it around my neck. I could not see it on me, but I felt it gently resting on the front of my collarbone and it felt right. I opened the letter.

Jan, t'ankshi!

Time for me to go. I am pleased you seem so happy, Steve is a great guy, and what a treasure you have with that little one. Thank you for allowing me to stay and reconnect. The necklace is for you, and I wish I had brought something for James Jab...great name! The Lakota tribe of South Dakota see the dragonfly as a symbol of renewal and life's continual change. I'll try to do better and keep in touch.

J.

That day at school, when I had a chance, I checked in the library and found *t'ankshi* translates from the Lakota language as *a man's young sister.* I touched the necklace, feeling its smooth silver, thinking if there was any creature who symbolized Jab's life, it was that one.

***

vii.

About a month after Jab left, another package was delivered to the house. When I opened it there was a brief note and a gift: a toy black and white horse, a "fighting stallion" for Jim. Jab's note said he thought Jim would like the horse. *Tell him I sometimes ride a horse out here that looks like that one,* he wrote, and when I gave the horse to Jim, he clung to it, played with it, and for a while, would not go to bed without it. I carefully examined the letter and the packaging, but there was no return address or telephone number, and I knew further contact would be at the mercy of Jab's decisions. I thought Jab said he was going east, or maybe south. I didn't know for sure. But he held true to his promise. At least for a while, and that year we received two postcards and a phone call.

One Sunday afternoon, when Steve had taken Jim to the nearby park and I was dozing over the tests I needed to grade, Jab called. I was glad to hear his voice and excited to tell him our news.

"When is the baby due?" he asked.

"In a couple months, at the start of summer break. Any chance you'll visit soon and meet your new niece or nephew?"

There was a hesitancy, and I could visualize Jab's head moving. "Probably not, but who knows? Maybe I'll get there again soon. And by the way, it's a niece. You and Steve are going to have a daughter."

I laughed. "Really? You can tell that from where you are? You must be psychic!"

I could hear Jab's smirk. "Maybe. But it's a girl. Sometimes I get these feelings," and we continued to talk for a time. I forgot to ask for a phone number or address, but I supposed he wouldn't have one to give anyway.

A couple weeks after that, I received a small envelope. Inside was a tiny pair of pink moccasins. They were beautifully made, but looking them over, I noticed a small hole in the bottom of one. I thought this was only an oddity until I read Jab's letter. He explained that according to some Native American traditions, a hole was created in the baby's first pair of shoes so that evil spirits would be fooled. This would protect the child because she could not travel far with a hole in the bottom of the moccasin. He was sure this child was a girl. I guessed he had a fifty-fifty chance of being correct. When Katherine was born, we called her *Kate* and put the moccasins on her. I still have the photograph of her wearing the hand-crafted pink moccasins. I put the pair away with Jab's letter. One day, perhaps her daughter will wear them.

The years passed, and Loretta, who had become a family friend, continued to help us by caring for Kate when Jim started school. Steve and I were busy, working our jobs, maintaining the house, raising two children, and I always seemed to be rushing from one place to another. Steve helped, but he was given a promotion and the responsibilities meant he had to put in additional long hours both at work and at home. One Friday, I had picked Jim up from kindergarten, Kate from Loretta's care, and traveled home looking forward to the weekend. I pulled into the driveway and saw that Jab was sitting on the front steps. His leather duffle bag was beside him, and a motorcycle was at the edge of the driveway.

I knew it was Jab although he looked different. He still had a beard, but his hair was short and salt-and-peppered. He was even thinner and looked tired. There were lines around his eyes, but they smiled when he looked at me, and I hugged him as I held Kate. He moved back and looked at her. Then he saw Jim and spoke to him.

"Hello Jimmy! Remember me? Been a while," and he looked at me and then at Kate. "I knew this one would be a girl. How are you, Jan? So glad to see you. Mind if I stay a while?"

Of course he was welcome, and all of us moved into the house where Jim and Kate were given a snack at the table. I poured cold water for Jab. The kids munched as they examined this stranger. Jim didn't seem to recognize his uncle, but as Jab and I talked, he ran to his room and came back out holding something behind his back. He held it up to Jab who grinned when he saw black and white horse he had sent him.

"Yep, that's *Tadita*, the horse I used to ride. The name *Tadita* means *one who runs*, and he sure did. Did you name your horse, Jimmy?"

Jim shook his head, afraid to speak, and Jab held out his hand. The horse was placed into it, and Jab held it up towards the sky. Jim watched as my brother intoned, "I honor you as *Tadita, one who runs,* and you belong to Jimmy. There," and he handed the toy back, "now you have a special name for your special stallion. Do you remember it?"

"Tadita!" said Jim, and the two smiled at each other, connecting with each other. Then Jim ran up to his room to play with his newly christened toy. I was surprised he remembered and was happy he did. Jab and I talked. He helped to ready dinner and told me about what he was doing, the things he had seen, the people he knew. I listened, and as he talked, I realized he told me little about himself. His stories were just that. It was as though he didn't want me to know about him, about his personal affairs, his innermost thoughts, his important experiences. I didn't press him, but simply listened and asked pertinent questions. I spoke about my life to him. About Steve and Jim and Kate. About my teaching and hopes and plans and wishes. I didn't hide my sentiments or views. I had nothing to conceal.

Jab had to sleep on the pull-out couch in the downstairs room we used as a catch-all space since the room he previously stayed in was now Kate's. But he didn't mind. "Believe me, I've slept on many floors and even outside plenty of times. This is great, Jan," he commented, and I made up his bed there.

On the following Monday when we went back to work and school, Jab continued to sleep. I left him a note on the kitchen counter and told him we would be home later; we'd take the kids and do some grocery shopping, and that's what happened. This time, there was no large wad of cash Jab pulled out of his pocket to pay for the bags of food. It didn't matter to me, but he seemed uncomfortable about it, and that gave me some insight to his financial affairs. I would be right about that and would learn more some days later.

He stayed for a little over a week. The kids, especially Jim, got used to him being around. When we returned home from school, Jim would run in to find Jab and settle next to him, answering Jab's questions and talking about whatever came up. The days passed, and I was glad Jab was with us. The following Sunday evening found us sitting in the back yard talking quietly. Kate and Jim were in bed and Steve was finishing up a report for work, and I was happy to just sit and be with my brother. I had been thinking about saying something to him and decided this was the time.

"Jab," I began, "I have a suggestion. I talked with Steve about this, and he agrees with me. Why don't you stay here with us? We can reorganize that back room. You're near forty now, and I know that traveling and living the life you wanted has been your dream, but we would welcome you here. You're talented and capable of doing many things, and you could easily find a job. There are lots of opportunities. And if you didn't want to live here, you could get an apartment close by. We'd love for you to stay and watch your nephew and niece grow. They love having you here. Remember: *There's no place like home*. What do you think?"

Jab looked out into the yard and then down at the ground. He took some time before he answered. "Thanks, Jan. I know I would be welcomed here, and I appreciate it. The best I can promise is…maybe. Someday. But not now. There are things I want to see and do, and while I would love to watch Jimmy and Katie grow and learn, I don't think it's in the cards for me. Not yet," and then he smiled at me. "I know you don't understand, and sometimes I don't either. It's just the way. *My life…ought to be a perpetual transcending, a progression from stage to stage…*" and he stopped.

I thought for a moment. "From *The Glass Bead Game?*"

He nodded. "Yes. And now I have something delicate and uncomfortable to ask of you, and I hesitate to ask, but…" he stopped and looked down and sighed.

I waited. And I waited some more.

"I need some money, Jan. I hate to ask, and I'm embarrassed about it, but I need to have something so I can get back. If it were possible for me to stay and work for a while, I would, but I can't stay here, on your kindness anymore."

"You are welcome to stay here, and money is not a problem, Jab. How much do you need?"

"A couple hundred. Two hundred would be great, if you could spare that much."

"After school tomorrow, I'll stop at the bank. Are you sure that's enough?"

"Yes, Jan. And it's a loan. I'll get it back to you. I promise."

I shook my head. "Unimportant. You know, when the old house was sold with the furniture and other things, Steve and I used part of the money, but we also saved part of it. It's yours, and you can have it."

"No, I don't want it. Just what I asked you for. As a loan."

We didn't talk much after that, but sat and watched the night. There were some fireflies that were beginning to show, and we talked about little things, nothing of importance. We sat and allowed any thoughts and questions we had to disappear into the darkness, to melt in silence and inaction.

The next day, after school and before I picked up Kate, I drove to the bank. Jim held my hand as we walked in and I withdrew three thousand dollars from the account. I had told Steve I was doing this, and he only said, "Well, that's fair." After dinner that night, I gave the large envelope filled with cash to Jab and told him it was his. He whispered his thanks and put it in his room, and we all sat in the front room and watched television and didn't speak much that evening. When we went to bed, Jab said he was going to stay up and watch an old movie. He said he would turn out the lights and make sure everything was shut and locked.

The following morning, Jab was still asleep when we left for work and school. I thought we would grill some burgers for dinner that night and stopped for some supplies at the grocery store before I picked up Kate. When we finally got home, Jab's motorcycle wasn't there. He had left. We went into the house, and Jim called for him, but silence answered. I kept the kids busy with their crayons, coloring books, and a snack as I emptied the bags and got a dinner ready for four and not five. When I had some time, I went into the back room to look around. The couch was moved back in place, the pillows were stacked, the bed blankets folded. On the couch cushion was the large envelope I had given Jab the night before, and in it was the cash. Except for two hundred dollars. Jab had written on the front: *Just a loan. Thanks. J.*

Kate was younger and didn't miss her uncle too much, but Jim cried when he realized Uncle Jab was gone. He wanted to see him. Was he coming back? Could we call him? Why did he leave? Where did he go? *Tadita* missed him, and so did Jim. I wiped his tears and tried to comfort him. How do you explain transiency to a child? How can he understand the wandering life? I didn't understand it myself, and had I known I would never see my brother alive again, I would have sobbed with my son.

***

viii.

Time moves quickly with a family. Soon Kate was in school;
elementary school and junior high were busy years, then both graduated
eighth grade and went to high school, and college was next for Jim. Life
sounds hum-drum and uneventful when stated like that, but it wasn't.
There were vacations to Florida and Maine and one memorable trip to
Hawaii. Memorable because Kate fell and cracked her ankle, and we
had to stay in Hawaii a week longer than we had planned. There could
be worse places to be stuck. There was T-Ball, Little League, soccer
teams, and then Jim wanted to be a Cub Scout but hated Boy Scouts, and
Kate wanted nothing to do with Brownies and cried when her best friend
decided to join. Friends came and went, and there were fights and sleep-
overs and backyard tents which fell at two in the morning when a sudden
rain drenched the four girls sleeping inside. Some loveable pet kittens
turned into cats who refused to honor their litter box, and a beloved
pet dog was buried in the backyard amidst sobs and tears which were
eased by the promise of additional pets. A series of cars came and went,
and a few accidents happened. Wakes and funerals were attended, and
Halloween costumes were agonized over while Christmas decorations
were scotch-taped to the walls and when removed, took with them small
strips of painted wall. Neighbors moved, and summer parties were held,
and autumn science projects were worried about and fussed over. And
in all these years, in the normality of family life and the profusion of
passing passions and vacillating views, only a handful of times was
communication in any form received from Jab.

Once he left that last time, he seemed to be more attentive to us,
to his family. For a while. A couple postcards addressed to *Master Jimmy
of the Family Henderson* were received. One of them had a picture of
a black and white stallion which looked like Tadita, and Jim insisted
it be tucked into the corner of his dresser mirror where he could view
it daily. It's still there. General postcards to all of us were sent from
various places: Missouri, Arkansas, Tennessee, and none of them said
much of importance. For the first couple of years, packages for Jim and
Kate would arrive at strange dates, never Christmas or birthdays, but
seemingly whenever Jab thought to send them. They would contain gifts
which were appropriate: old arrowheads for Jim and cornhusk dolls for
Kate; and gifts which were not meant for children: shot glasses, magnets,
tea towels with various states outlined on them. Whatever the gifts were,
they were greeted with yelps of delight. Kate used the tea towels to wrap
around her cornhusk dolls, and Jim trapped various insects under the shot
glasses, so all received items were serviceable.

Phone calls came in periodically, usually on Sunday afternoons, and Jab spoke to both Jim and Kate on the occasions they were in the house. The calls were perfunctory and brief with little of consequence said. But my anxiousness was eased when I knew he was still around, and I ended each call with a query about his next visit and the reminder that *there was no place like his home*, and Jab always responded, "Don't know. Sometime, maybe." I had to abide by his answer. And as the years passed, there were fewer postcards and almost no phone calls, and the packages stopped coming, and although I continued to worry about my brother, I had come to accept, almost accept, his nomadic lifestyle, his vagabond ways, his uncertain future. And then years passed and nothing had been heard from my brother. No packages, no phone calls, no postcards, and no way for me to get in touch with him.

It was the summer before Jim's senior year and Kate's junior year, and they were busy with summer jobs and activities with friends. I just finished teaching a summer session at the high school and was looking forward to resting for a few weeks. Steve and I talked about taking a long weekend trip with the kids somewhere close, maybe a nice hotel with a pool and a great restaurant. I also needed to prepare for the new fall class I would teach, and we were attempting to do some remodeling of the kitchen. We were taping it and readying it for painting, and I needed to get out and look for a new stove. There were vegetables in the garden which needed to be harvested, and Steve was working during the evenings at his mother's house, refinishing her table and chairs. I needed to corral the kids and take them shopping to get a few new things for the fall school season. Jim had another growth spurt and he needed new shoes and clothes, and while all this was going on, the phone call came.

A message was left on the machine, and when I came home from my last day of teaching summer school, I didn't play it until I had changed my clothes, poured some iced tea, and gathered the mail. When I got around to playing it, there was a message from a hospital in South Bend, Indiana. A woman spoke, "Is this the number for Janet Henderson? I am Dr. Helen Williams from the Grace Hospital in South Bend, Indiana. I need to speak to you about your brother, Jonathan Boyd, who is here in the hospital. Please call me back as soon as possible," and there was a phone number. I called immediately, and when I got in touch with Dr. Williams, the news was bad.

Jab had been in a motorcycle accident on a highway near South Bend and was seriously injured. At least that is what I was told over the telephone. I was asked to come to the hospital, and as soon as I hung up, I called Steve at work. We immediately arranged for his mother to stay with Jim and Kate who were not pleased they had a babysitter at their ages. That's what they said, but I was in no mood to argue with them. We worked fast, packing clothes, getting ready cash, gassing up the car, and gathering papers the doctor told me to bring, not that I had many. I did have Jab's birth certificate, and although I wasn't asked to bring that, I didn't have anything else she asked me for: insurance cards, an ID, medical records, other items I assumed Jab had. We left early that evening and later that night, when we got to the hospital, we were taken into a small room where we waited for Dr. Williams. She was professional and kind, but her compassion didn't help when she told us that Jab had died in the ambulance on his way to the hospital. She couldn't give us that news over the phone. Death requires a face-to-face conference to assist in mitigating sorrow. It doesn't work.

Jab's motorcycle was destroyed. His leather duffel bag was taken from the accident scene and stored away. It would be given to us. Jab's wallet contained no ID or driver's license or insurance cards of any kind, but there was some cash and a note he had written. It gave his name, date of birth, and social security number along with the information that I was his sister. My phone number was included, and that is how the hospital knew to call me. Just like Jab. He apparently had driven for years without a license or insurance, believing those things were unnecessary.

I asked to see him, and Steve and I were taken to the hospital morgue where his body was resting. He looked even thinner. He had shaved, and there was no beard, and for the first time in years, I saw his face and realized he looked like our father, and that, more than anything, caused me to cry. His hair was longer but now it was more salt than pepper, and except for some bruises on his face, he didn't look like he had been in an accident. Apparently, his insides were mangled and horribly damaged and many bones were broken. The hospital was kind and allowed us to stay with him and grieve. Once we left him, we were sent to several offices where there were piles of paperwork to complete, bills to settle, and a decision about what to do with Jab had to be made. Cremation was the best choice, and we were grateful for the assistance and advice provided by the hospital.

Neither Steve nor I realized we would be staying in a hotel in South Bend for most of a week. It made little sense to travel home when there was always something else to take care of: papers to fill out and file, phone calls to make, lines in which to wait. The funeral director the hospital recommended to us was understanding and helped to facilitate what is usually a longer process. Steve communicated with his office over the phone, and I spoke with Steve's mother and the kids daily, and once everything had been done, we packed the car to travel home. I held the urn with Jab's ashes during the entire trip. We forgot to ask about the duffel bag, and a phone call came about a week later with the box containing his bag a month or so after that.

I carefully placed Jab on the upper shelf of my closet, pushing him back so that he would rest against the wall and not fall. The new school year was about to begin, and there were so many tasks to complete that I had little time to mourn. But each day, as I got dressed and placed the silver dragonfly around my neck, resting it on my collarbone, I thought about Jab. I wondered about him and his life. I wished I knew more and became sad that I would never be aware of what he did with his life, or where he lived, or who, if anyone, he loved. I remembered him with Jim, holding Tadita up to the sky, naming him; my son looking up at the black and white stallion, grinning at the faux seriousness of the impromptu ceremony, and when Jab placed the toy back into Jim's arms, they smiled at each other. Before I left for school one day, I peeked into Jim's bedroom wondering if the toy horse was still around. It was. Jim had set it in the corner of his dresser situated under the postcard, the one addressed to *Master Jimmy of the Family Henderson*, the one tucked into the corner of his dresser mirror where he could view it daily.

***

ix.

The box remained in the corner of the front closet for months, and while I hadn't forgotten about it, I wasn't yet ready to examine the contents. Autumn came and went, and so did winter, and it was during the following year's spring break when I decided the time had arrived. It was a midweek morning, and I was home alone. Steve was at work, Kate was out with friends for the day, and Jim was working at his part-time job, earning additional money for college in the fall. The box had been left in the closet intact. I pulled it out from the corner into the hallway and opened it. The only thing in it was the familiar duffle bag. I broke down the box and carried it out to the garbage recycling bin. Then I came back to the hallway. I didn't want to have anyone walk in on me as I opened the duffle bag, so I carried it upstairs to the bedroom and shut the door.

This action made me feel like I was doing something illicit, something illegal, and I tried to shake off that feeling. This was my brother's bag, and what did I expect to find in it? Drugs? Pornography? A weapon? Maybe. I didn't know, and I hesitated. Then I picked the bag up and went over to the corner of the room where I sat in the easy chair. It didn't seem very heavy, and I wondered if it contained all of Jab's worldly belongings. Were there other bags or boxes stored away in a room or a house or an apartment somewhere? Did an unknown person have access to Jab's books or writings or clothes or valuables? I would never know unless there were directions or an address or a phone number in the bag. I reached down to unbuckle and unzip it.

I pulled out clothes. They seemed to be clean, and there weren't that many of them. Some tee-shirts and a pair of jeans, underwear and socks, a baseball cap that I thought I recognized, two bandanas, an old sweater, and a worn jacket. I looked at each piece, shook them out, and examined all the pockets, but there was nothing in them. I didn't know what I would do with them, but later, I decided, I would wash the clothes. Maybe the thrift store could use them. I examined the bag and there were two things left: a book and another bag. This bag was a cloth one, the kind someone would purchase at a souvenir shop to give as a gift. There was a nature scene on the front with flowers and some bees and an embroidered cursive saying which exclaimed: *What a Wonderful Day!* Inside were some items, but I put the second bag to the side and looked first at the book.

It was the copy of Hesse's *The Glass Bead Game*. The cover was blue, and as I thumbed through it, it was the one I kept from the cleaning of his room at Mom's house; the one I gave to him the last time I saw him. I shook out the pages thinking there might be a note of some kind stuck between them, but nothing fell out. Because I hadn't read the book the last time I had it in my possession, I wasn't sure if additional notes had been added to what was previously there. I thought this time, I would take time and read the book. Maybe I would find out something about Jab; perhaps it could help me understand him and his life and his choices. I put it to the side and held up the cloth bag. There were a few items inside, some wrapped in ripped brown paper. I took out one at a time: a grab-bag of sorts.

The first thing I pulled out was a small plastic bag containing a photograph, a somewhat faded old Polaroid photo. I examined it. Jab, a much younger Jab, was standing with his arm about a woman I did not recognize, and off to the side stood an unfamiliar man. The woman was looking at Jab who was looking towards the camera, and they were both smiling. The other man had a serious, almost angry look. The background was not familiar. The photo had been taken outside, and what looked like a barn was off to one side. I could see a fence and some picnic items, so it could have been a farm or a wooded area or someone's backyard. I turned it over and there was just a date, *1970*, written on the back. No names, no identification of any sort, but this photo was important enough that Jab kept it for thirty years. The date would have been after he left the house the first time, and I stared at the picture of Jab for a long time, trying to see what was in his eyes, examining his expression, hoping to determine anything about this man whose bloodline I shared but knew nothing about. I put the picture back into the bag and placed it to the side.

I took out the other items one at a time, lining them up on the window sill, allowing the sun to shine behind and around them. I examined the things closely, and then investigated the cloth bag finding one more thing. It was a ten-dollar bill that had been folded up. I opened it up and as I turned it over, I saw that someone (Didn't look like Jab's handwriting.) had written on it in red ink: *Won at Hopper's.* I placed it next to the other things and looked over the miscellany before me. A rogue's gallery of curious items which were somehow important enough to Jab that he wrapped them and kept them in his duffel bag. His secret cache. Perhaps the answer to who he was, to why he traveled, to where he drifted.

I counted the items: a beaded keychain, a pack of playing cards, an old Swiss army knife, a broken watch, drumsticks, three pens held together with a rubber band, a woman's scarf, and unwrapped and thrown in the bottom, a refrigerator magnet. Counting the photograph and the ten-dollar bill, there were ten things; ten insights into the brother I didn't know; ten glimpses into his life; ten quirky, baffling, bewildering, perplexing artifacts which held secrets I would never, could never, discover. There they were, lined up, waiting to tell the story that I would never hear.

I sat in front of them for a long time. I picked up the pens. They were a dark forest green and smudged gold printing was on the sides but most of the words were rubbed off. I tried to discern what they said and could make out some letters: *El,* and the word *Ranch,* and more letters, *olf,* but not much else was visible. I held the woman's scarf up to the light. It was maroon and gold, and what looked like calla lilies edged it. Bits of green were meant to stand for leaves, but there was no tag which would allow knowledge of its place of origin. I sniffed at it, thinking I might smell a perfume, but if there had been any, it had evaporated into the air long ago. I took out a pair of drumsticks held together by a rubber band, the beaded keychain which looked like a twin to the one Jab had gifted Steve years ago, a broken watch whose crown no longer worked because it just moved back and forth unable to adjust the hands or set the time, the rusted Swiss knife, and a magnet which claimed *There's No Place Like Home.* The pack of playing cards was complete. I counted them, and there were fifty-two cards, all intact in what I assumed was their original container, a worn cardboard box. These were things that a child might keep in a treasure box. But Jab was no child, and this was no treasure.

Finally, I took each item, rewrapping some in the wrinkled brown paper, and placed all back into the cloth bag. *What a Wonderful Day!* The decorated bag was laid back inside the duffle bag, and I walked over to my closet and stored the whole lot into the far recess just below the shelf upon which Jab's urn was stored. Owner and owner's things. I leaned down and picked up the blue-covered book and set it on the top of my dresser. Then I gathered Jab's clothes, opened the bedroom door, and walked down the stairs into the laundry room. I checked once more through the pockets before I washed the clothes. Nothing. I didn't make a mistake the first time. They were empty. I loaded the washer and started the process, putting his baseball cap to the side and hanging up the jacket which I thought I might take to the cleaners. I stood there for a few minutes trying to decide whether I was relieved or disappointed by my morning's activity, but I couldn't decide, so I walked to the fridge and poured myself a glass of iced tea.

The late morning proclaimed one of those perfect spring days, the kind you would like to bottle and then uncork during the depths of snowy winter. *What a Wonderful Day!* I stood at the screen door and looked towards the back yard where I saw the weedy vegetable patch which called to be cleaned and readied for planting. In the kitchen, leaning against the napkin holder on the table was a pile of bills waiting to be paid, and the breakfast dishes listed crookedly to one side in the sink demanding attention. I examined the waiting tasks once more. Then purposefully ignoring them, I resolutely and quickly walked up the stairs to the bedroom, marched to the dresser, and grabbed the blue-covered book.

I returned to the laundry room where I took Jab's worn baseball cap and jammed it on my head. In the kitchen, I picked up the glass of iced tea, carefully opened the back screen door, and walked out to the patio. Placing my glass on top of the patio table and pulling out the chair, I sat down. Then I adjusted the baseball cap so the brim would shade my eyes. With a last glance at the unheeded vegetable patch, I opened the blue-covered book and began to read.

***

III.

His
Things

If only there were a dogma to believe in. Everything is contradictory, everything tangential; there are no certainties anywhere. Everything can be interpreted one way and then again interpreted in the opposite sense.

1. Photograph

Serenely let us move to distant places
And let no sentiments of home detain us.

Jab finished replacing the bearings on the steering head and wiped his hands on the oily rag he had been using to clean them. He looked at Mark and nodded.

"Should start fine, now. Go on and give it a try."

Mark started the motorcycle and listened for a second before he steered it out to the road and drove around for a few minutes. Jab watched as he came back.

Mark nodded as he stopped and hopped off. "It's better, but it still vibrates a bit. Check for loose bolts. I'll call Henry and let him know his bike is fixed. Meri is making lunch, and I didn't eat yet, so I'm going to grab something. See you in a few," and he walked to the side door of the large farmhouse and entered.

The late spring day was warm as Jab completed his job, checked out the bike one more time, and went into the kitchen to wash up and eat lunch. He and Mark sat at the battered kitchen table taking large bites of the grilled cheese sandwiches Meri made and placed in front of them. She opened the ancient refrigerator, pulled out three bottles of soda for them, and after handing them out, sat down, pulling the newspaper towards her. Mark and Jab discussed the rest of the work which needed to be done, and Meri glanced through the paper as she ate her sandwich.

About three months before, Jab, who was biking through southern Illinois, stopped at a bar in a small town for a beer and a sandwich which is where he met Mark. They struck up a discussion about traveling and biking, and when they spoke about Jab's motorcycle, Mark asked if he kept up his own repairs, which he did. Deciding Jab might be helpful, Mark asked if he would accompany him to his farmhouse to look over an old car he couldn't seem to get started. They left the bar and went to examine the car. Jab lifted the hood, adjusted a few things, and after additional tweaking, the car started.

"Great," admired Mark, "You know about cars."

"Had one like this," replied Jab, "and sold it for my bike."

They continued to talk, and Mark told Jab he could camp out at his farmhouse if he wanted. Jab took him up on the offer. After a week of helping work on the vehicles parked around the yard, Mark suggested Jab remain to help him with his repair business. There was no other place to be, no hurry to move on, and this offer was as good as any, so Jab agreed and moved inside to one of the bedrooms. After a month of watching him work successfully on the various bikes and cars needing repairs, Mark added a line advertising *Motorcycle Repairs* to the large wooden sign in the front. He thought it would increase his business, and once word got around, it did. Mark and Jab were kept busy.

When traveling bikers had vehicle problems they couldn't handle on their own, *Mark's Repairs* would be suggested as a place they could rely on to obtain parts and help. The fact that the large farmhouse could also serve as a lodging place while repairs were being made was extra inducement for them to make the off-road visit when cruising down one of the major highways surrounding Waterville, Illinois. Mark didn't mind strangers staying, as long as they were polite, caused no trouble, helped when they could, and cleaned up after themselves. There were plenty of rooms in the house and space outdoors if camping was preferred.

It was in this way Meri appeared. She and a friend, Jake, were traveling in his VW Beetle which was having problems. Having heard about Mark's place, they pulled in. Loose wiring and a new starter solved the issue, and they stayed on the farm for the five days it took to get the parts. Once repairs were completed, Jake was ready to leave, but Meri wasn't. She liked the freedom being on her own provided, and decided that Jake was being too clingy. Too possessive. Jake took off leaving Meri behind. She found a part-time job at one of the two bars in town, agreed to do some cooking and cleaning at the farmhouse, and settled into the bedroom on the top floor.

Waterville, Illinois, in Monroe County, was about ninety miles north of St. Louis and a couple hundred miles southwest of Chicago. It was a small community with the two bars, a couple diners, the usual feed and hardware business, and a general store on Market Street, the main route through town. A grocery store, post office, library, and a few other small businesses took up space on the cross road, Prairie Street, which was also Illinois Route 156. Some churches, the elementary school and the high school were placed near each other, and of the twelve thousand people or so who made up the surrounding community, most were farmers whose major crops were soybeans, corn, and wheat. Some chicken and cattle farms were close, and a couple pig farms could be located by their aroma. When there was free time, when farming duties allowed, Waterville families would visit Springfield which was thirty miles east, take a ride to the western border of the state where the Mississippi River offered scenic adventures, or visit relatives in that far away town of Chicago. It was a quiet life, a busy life, and Jab took to it. He didn't know how long he would stay at Mark's, but there was nothing pressing him to move on. Waterville suited him for the time being.

He and Mark got along. Mark was fair in paying Jab what he could and when he was able. No rent was asked, and food and supplies, when needed, were bought by whomever was going to town to shop. Living was simple and relaxed. The men shared their mechanical knowledge and techniques and spent free time discussing philosophy and politics and the meaning of life in general. Whenever there were additional travelers at the farm, nights around a campfire outside, far to the back of the house, were enjoyed, and the passing of items for a sip or a toke was acceptable. Or not. No one was forced or stopped, and ideas and substances were shared. It was the freedom Jab found that was so addictive.

People drifted in and out of the farmhouse. Some were repeat visitors. A few stayed for a couple of weeks before moving on. Others stayed for a night or two and were never seen again. Most were friendly and careful and helped around the farm by mowing the grass or cleaning the rooms or cooking meals and providing food. Rarely did Mark need to rely on the Waterville police to help move a troublemaker along, but because Mark had grown up in the town and lived in the farmhouse deeded to him by his dead grandparents, the authority figures in the town were his friends. Or at least his acquaintances. Sometimes, after removing the offending visitors and making sure they left the town, the police would return and stay for a while, discussing life and gossiping with Mark and Jab. It all worked out.

During the winter when there were fewer repairs to make, Mark and Jab, and eventually Meri would spend time playing cards and watching old movies on the television, when the reception was reliable. They would discuss the books which they had read and ponder the ideas of Hesse and Huxley and Ram Dass and Castaneda. At times, Jab would play the old guitar Mark stored in the corner of the living room, and the others would listen to him sing. If the weather was particularly bad, either Mark or more often Jab, would drive to town using whichever car or truck was currently running, and take Meri to her job at the bar. If she had to work the late-night shift, Jab would usually pick her up just after midnight. The two men kept an amiable distance from Meri who made it obvious that she only wanted to be friends with them although she and Jab shared a marginal flirtation. The summer passed; the winter came, and then it was spring again. Wayfarers returned.

The news about Mark's repair shop and hospitality spread and additional travelers took advantage of the expertise and friendship offered. Mark and Jab were busy, working at fixing stalled cars, rusted trucks, vibrating motorcycles. Broken toasters, untuned lawnmowers, and the favorite coffee pot needing adjustments occasionally appeared at the workshop, and time passed. Someone bought and left a Polaroid camera at the farm, and, when film was available, it became a habit to take pictures of visitors and post them on the old refrigerator in the kitchen. Mark and Jab and Meri appeared in many of the photos, and repeat visitors hunted until they found the photo of the last time they stayed at the farm. It was a friendly space to stay for a time, and Jab was content.

The passing flirtation between Jab and Meri became more serious. At least on Jab's part. He would often visit Meri at work, nurse a beer or two and talk to her when times were slow. He waited for her to finish the late shift and drove her home. He looked after her. Some nights, when the bar was devoid of drinkers, the two of them discussed their lives, their hopes, their experiences. Meri was a good listener, and Jab was a better talker, and they got along.

"So, your sister is much younger than you?"

"She's ten years younger," explained Jab as he sipped the beer. "She's smart, and I hope she'll go to college and do better than I did. I think about her and my parents, and I've been thinking I should take a ride back to see them. I might do that now that I've got a decent motorcycle. I need to take it out on the road."

Jab had bought an almost new bike from one of the farmers who came into the bar. The bike was dependable and well-engineered, and he had worked on it to increase its reliability. Jab was anxious to take the Honda out for a long ride. He was also feeling guilty about being away and not seeing his sister and parents in a long time. He sent them some postcards and called a few times just to let them know he was OK, but now that the weather was good, he was feeling restless.

"That's a good idea, Jab," agreed Meri. "Maybe you should think about a trip."

Jab did think about it. A couple weeks later, he packed and prepared to leave for the Chicago suburb where he had left his family. His sister was a teenager. His parents were getting older. He decided he should see them. Before leaving, he spoke to Mark.

"Listen, Mark, do you mind if I give Jan your phone number? Just in case something happens and she needs to call. I'll make sure she knows it's only for emergencies."

"Sure," said Mark, "That's fine. I guess that means you're coming back?"

"Yep. Be gone a few weeks. Are you going to be OK with just you and Meri?"

"Yep. Ride safe."

Jab packed his duffel bag, strapped it to the back of the bike, and said his good-byes. Meri and Mark watched as he took off, waving him away. Mark turned back to go to the workshop where he would finish tinkering with a broken lawnmower. Meri stood for a longer time, shading her eyes with her hand, and watching Jab until she couldn't see him or hear the thrumming of his bike.

***

Some weeks later Jab returned. It was late, and Mark was inside watching television. A couple of visitors had set up their tent to the back of the farmhouse, and it was a quiet night. Jab parked his bike, unstrapped his duffel bag, and walked through the side door.

"Hey, I'm back," he spoke to Mark. "Everything fine? Seems pretty quiet around here."

"Have a good visit? Yeah, not too many people around lately. Glad you're here and safe. There's a whole lot of small items to repair, and I could use your help. There's some stew left if you're hungry."

"Thanks. I'm good. Stopped a while ago to eat," and Jab sat down in the old tatty chair next to Mark. "Where's Meri? Working late tonight? I'll go and pick her up later."

Mark looked at him and shook his head. "Meri left about a week ago."

Jab stared at him. "Left? Is she coming back? Where did she go? Why?"

Mark shrugged. "A couple girls came by in an old car that needed work. They stayed for a few days while I worked on it, and Meri seemed to like them. The three of them spent time talking. When they left, they were headed west, probably to Texas, and Meri said she was going with them. She said it was time to go and to tell you she would miss you. She also said she'd call and check in once she was settled somewhere. That's all I know. No one stays long here. You're an exception and so was Meri. Maybe she'll be back sometime. But she cleaned her room and took everything with her, so who knows?" and Mark turned back to the television.

Jab sat for a while before getting up and going to his room. He unpacked, took a quick shower, and laid in his bed in the dark for a long time, staring up to the ceiling. Finally, he fell asleep.

He was up early the next morning. He went to the kitchen to make a pot of coffee and while he waited for it, he stared at the Polaroid photographs scattered across the refrigerator. He picked one up and examined it carefully. It was a picture of Meri and him. They were standing together and his arm was around her, and Mark was off to the side. Meri was looking at Jab, and he was looking towards the camera, and they were both smiling. Mark looked serious, almost angry, although Jab couldn't remember why, and the background showed the old barn off to one side with the fence and some picnic items present. Jab remembered that day. It was last summer when a large group had been present. Earlier that day a decision was made to have a cookout. A volleyball net was set up and a game organized. Food and drink were shared, and later that evening, as everyone sat around a large fire, Meri brought out the old guitar for Jab to play. There was singing and laughing, and as the darkness grew and the fire died, people began to drift off to their tents and sleeping bags. Meri and Jab stayed up later than the others, talking and confiding in each other. When the fire was out, they went back into the farmhouse to quietly continue their conversation. Eventually they fell asleep wrapped in blankets. Next to each other, but separately. In the morning he helped in the kitchen while Meri made a tower of pancakes for breakfast, and everyone came in to eat. Jab summoned up the images.

He held the photograph in his hands and stared at it. It was not replaced on the crowded refrigerator. It wouldn't be missed. There were so many. He took the square into his bedroom and pulled out the duffel bag from under the bed. Unzipping the hidden side pocket, he stored the picture in it, then returned it to underneath the bed, went back to the kitchen, poured himself a cup of the hot coffee, and went out to the workshop to examine the items which needed repair.

Mark

After my dad died and then my mom got sick, she and I moved in to the old farmhouse with my grandparents. Mom just got sicker. She didn't make it, so Grandma and Grandpa raised me from the time I was ten. I lived with them, grew up, and took care of them, burying them both. I was by myself at the farm afterwards, but when people started to travel through and ask if they could stay on the farm for a night or two, I took to the company, and that's how the farm got the reputation as a safe place for travelers, young travelers, to stay. Most visitors who came by didn't remain for longer than a night or two, although some did return, and it was OK with me. I rarely had any problems, and when I did, I'd call Frankie or Joe who were on the local police force. We went to grade school and high school together, and they often hung out here. In fact, when Frankie married Nora, another high school friend, their wedding was held here at the back of the house, and we had a great time afterwards at their reception in the side yard next to the barn. Anyway, with people coming and going, I was never lonely.

It was Grandpa who taught me how to fix stuff. He had a small farm and grew some corn and vegetables, but he always said he was not meant to be a farmer. Instead, he kept a repair business, and he showed me what to do and how to fix things in the large workshop fully stocked with tools. I learned plenty from him and took over the trade and the business after he died. There were always toasters or lamps or lawn mowers and vacuums to fix, and I was able to do some basic repairs for cars or trucks too. There were lots of neighbors who didn't want to spend the money or have the time to take their vehicles to some expensive shop, so they brought their stuff to me. I was able to get them going, although I was never a real mechanic. I learned a lot from Jab when he joined me. He had knowledge and could fix most of the problems. He was a good teacher, and I was glad for his help.

I called him a *teacher*, but he never thought of himself as one. We had lots of talks late at night, and while I was never much of a reader and could barely get through the high school books and readings I had been assigned, Jab read plenty and told me about the stuff he learned. He went to college but said he never graduated. Said he learned more from the books he read and the discussions he and his friends held than from the classes which he claimed were boring. *Stodgy* was what he called them, and I had never heard of that word, but it sounded like it fit. He had ideas about what life should be, and he tried to explain them to me.

"Life is about learning," he said one night when it was raining and I had the fireplace going to get the chill out. "And that's what I want to do. Don't think I'll ever have a steady job like my father has. In fact, that's been a problem. We had lots of arguments about what I should do and be, about my education and responsibilities," and he was silent.

"My dad died when I was really young," I answered, "so we never had those arguments. But Grandma and I had some heated discussions. Grandpa told me to just listen and nod, and be quiet. He said that's how he did it all those years," and we both laughed. "I never could be silent like he told me to. Did your mother ever argue with you?"

"She was the peacemaker. She tried to get us to understand each other, but it didn't take. One thing led to another with my dad. We would begin a conversation about education, usually mine, then it turned to politics and religion, and it always ended in a fight," and Jab shook his head. "I wanted him to read some of the books I had, but he refused. He said that there were no books that would change his mind about his beliefs, so I just stopped suggesting it to him. By the way, did you ever read this one?" and he pulled out a book that was by his side and threw it to me.

"*The Teachings of Don Juan. A Yaqui Way of Knowledge,*" I read the title and shrugged. "Nope, but if there's something important it can teach me, I'll give it a try. Not really a reader, Jab."

Jab shrugged. "Well, take it if you want. Probably reading little bits at a time might be easier for this one."

I put the book to the side and looked at him. "Maybe you should go back and finish college. You seem like you'd be a good teacher. Probably better than the ones you had."

"I'm done with formal education," and Jab took a long swig of his beer. "I think it's more important to learn by being an apprentice, and that's what I intend to do: apprentice myself to those who can teach me something. Like you."

"Ha! Not much of a teacher here. Not sure I can tell you much. You seem to understand plenty about fixing stuff and knowing what to do. You taught me things that I didn't know about bikes and trucks. I think you got the roles mixed up."

Jab smiled and we were quiet for a time. I got up and went to the kitchen and brought back more beers, and we sat and sipped for a while.

I worked at the dials on the old television and tried to get something to come in but got nothing except noise and snow. The rain outside was the problem. Finally, I just stopped and turned it off. "Guess not tonight, Teach," I said.

Jab laughed. "Apprentice and teacher. Sometimes those roles are interchangeable."

That night we sat and talked and listened to the rain and the thunder, and it grew dark. I remember the rain softening and dripping on the windows making it seem like someone was constantly knocking to come in. In a while we stopped talking, and Jab reached over to grab the old guitar leaning against the corner. He tuned it up, strummed it, and played a song I had never heard, humming along with it. I listened, watching him, and wondering who he was and how he seemed to know so much. He really did but was never braggy or stuck-up about it. He was helpful, and I enjoyed his company for the time he stayed at the farmhouse.

Sometimes he left. He'd say that he was taking the bike for a ride and not to worry if he didn't return for a few days. I never knew where he went. He would come back and say he'd been out riding and looking around and thinking. When he got hungry, he'd try to find a place to get something to eat, and sometimes he said he just pulled up under a tree or a large road sign and sleep. He just seemed to get those spells where he was anxious and jumpy and needed to be away. He was usually fine when he came back. Like the riding and looking and thinking calmed him down. Made him peaceful again.

When Meri showed up and stayed for a time, I thought the two of them would become a couple. She seemed to calm him down too, make him want to stay at the farm and not travel around on those short trips he'd take. But Meri was pretty clear about wanting to be by herself. They did get along though, and I was surprised when she left with those two girls. It was almost like she waited for Jab to leave so she could too. Too bad. They seemed a good match.

After a long time helping me on the farm and working at The Watering Hole, he left for good. One night when it was rainy and I was by myself in the farmhouse, I picked up the book he had thrown to me that night and looked through it. I tried to read it, but never read all of it because it seemed confusing and strange. But I looked through it, and when I opened the front cover, I saw that he had copied something that I noted was underlined in the book. He wrote:

For me there is only the traveling on paths that have heart, on any path that may have heart, and the only worthwhile challenge is to traverse its full length—and there I travel looking, looking breathlessly.

I wonder about Jab. I wonder if he found that path that has heart. I wonder if he travels it looking breathlessly. Sure does sound like him.

2. Drumsticks

*Making music together is the best way for two people
to become friends. There is none easier. That is a fine thing.*

A new bar, set back into a wooded area, opened just outside the Waterville city limits, along Route 156. Years ago, it was a warehouse for a currently defunct company, and the inside space allowed for a large bar, a restaurant, and another room with a spacious stage where unknown and little-known bands and musicians could come to practice their art and expand their reputation. It was here that Jab began to work part-time. The repair business kept Mark busy, but lately, defective vehicles were scarce, and there didn't seem to be enough small broken toasters to keep the two of them occupied. Jab felt bad that he was inessential.

When the new place, *The Watering Hole Bar and Grill,* was being organized, Jab met and spoke to the owner and builder who hired him because of his expertise working with mechanical things. Jab did all sorts of work. He helped carry in the lumber and then assisted in creating the long wooden bar. He serviced some of the electrical fixtures, brought in food and bar supplies, placed them in their specified locations, and when the business opened, he stayed on, working where he was needed. If that meant filling in as a bartender, he learned how to mix drinks; if working as a fry cook when one didn't show up, he knew not to get burned; when he hooked up and managed the lighting for the stage, he adjusted it to the musicians' satisfaction. He caught on quickly and became useful and reliable, and the new owner of the place, Hank Fontaine, discovered he could count on him. Jab became the backstage crew, a crew of one, for the musicians who showed up. Generally, if they were large enough of a band, they had a roadie or two, and Jab just assisted. He found out quickly that musicians were picky about who carried and placed their gear and apparatus. If a single musician, usually a guitar playing singer, was the entertainment, he or she was grateful for Jab's help. He learned when to offer help and when to stand back. And as the part-time job became a full-time one, he knew there was a need to discuss things with Mark.

"Listen, Mark, I can still help with cars and bikes that come in. Most days I don't need to be at The Watering Hole until two or so in the afternoon. I don't want to leave you alone to work here. I know there's still stuff to fix, and I like doing it."

"Great. Right now, there are a couple bikes that need to be looked at. Things have slowed down, and I know you have a job now. Still appreciate the assistance."

Jab nodded. "Well, I'm earning some money now, and I want to be fair about pulling my load, so let's talk about what you'll charge for rent," and the two of them discussed it. Jab wasn't earning much, but he was paid in cash, and he felt obligated to Mark.

The Watering Hole became popular. Partly because there were few entertainment places like it in the area. Travelers were happy there was something to do between Springfield and St. Louis, and townspeople stopped by for the pub food and stayed for the beer and entertainment. Musicians and bands began to make the new venue a regular stop on their itinerary. Some of them would book a house gig, playing three or more times in a year, and Jab was available to assist in the smooth operation of the business.

He suggested to Hank that billboards along Route 156 could be obtained to advertise The Watering Hole. Hank was unsure about it because it was a costly endeavor, but soon discovered that the money spent was justified by the increased crowds at the establishment. Additional signage touting coming events was placed at the entrance, on the stage, in the restrooms, and business owners in the town were happy to display posters in their windows. Additional visitors increased their revenue, and The Watering Hole brought in the visitors. The thriving restaurant and music venue business pleased Hank who continued to rely on Jab's ideas and decisions. There was no lack of musicians and bands who wanted to be on the stage, and Jab became Hank's proxy when it came to choosing acts and organizing schedules. Several semi-known bands came to share their music with audiences. Most of the performers were making the circuit between southern Illinois and Missouri with a few traveling in and out of Indiana and Iowa, and Jab became familiar with the ones which were talented, popular, and the least likely to cause a fracas either in the venue, the town, or at the motels in which they stayed. The troublemakers were not allowed back. The popular, trustworthy musicians were. It was with one of these musicians Jab became friends. His name was Buzz.

The band was called The BeeStings, and when Jab questioned him about the name, Buzz, the drummer, and originator of the group claimed, "Blame it on a past girlfriend. Too expensive to change it now. Name is on all the posters." The first time they showed up, Jab offered to help the band carry in and set up their gear, but Buzz just laughed. "We need to do the set up, but here's my throne. Put it close to my drum cases," and he handed him the three-legged stool. Jab took the seat and placed it on the stage and watched as the remainder of the gear was brought in by the band.

Buzz walked over with the last case and began to remove his drums, set the brackets, tightened the wing nuts, and spoke to Jab. "So, what do you have for a backline?"

"Some amps, speakers, PA system. There is a piano I can get out here if you want. We don't have that much because we haven't been opened for live music that long, but are keeping track of what's needed. We do have some items ordered and are waiting for delivery, but I can show you what's available for your use."

Buzz nodded. "We have most of what we need. Traveling around, we can't get caught in a venue that has nothing. Let me finish up here and I'll look at it. Micky has his keyboard and amp, so leave the piano off the stage," and he continued to work.

The BeeStings made a loop between Chicago and St. Louis, playing small venues and college towns. The Watering Hole would be on their schedule every few months, and they became a popular draw for the business. When the band was in town, the members, except for Buzz, would stay at either the nearby Crosstown Inn or the Manor Motel. Buzz would travel to the farmhouse with Jab and along with Mark, would spend what remained of those nights talking and drinking and easing into a friendship. They argued about politics, discussed current metaphysical theories, and confessed their sins to each other. Periodically Jab would take the old guitar, and he and Buzz would make Mark laugh with the parodies they created. Buzz was never without a pair of drumsticks, and he would improvise rhythmic riffs on the wooden floor of the living room as accompaniment to Jab's guitar playing. They would stay in the shadowy room, immersed in their discussions and music, and when exhaustion settled, would curl up on the floor, wrapped in old quilts and blankets, gentle snores filling the space until the noon sun, acting as an alarm clock, woke them with an urgency for food and a shower, nudging them to begin the dwindling day.

Days, weeks, months progressed, and Jab was mostly untroubled. He continued at The Watering Hole, and on those mornings, when Mark needed him to help with a defective coffee pot or a malfunctioning motorcycle, he woke and worked at the task, content to fix what he could. He concentrated on his projects, focused on his undertakings, acknowledged the cycles of the moon and sun, willed himself to simply *be*. A slight stirring was recognized, a fitfulness, an irregularity in his being was detected, and while he said nothing to either Mark or Hank, he knew that a change was imminent, that an impending decision was pulsing at the back of his mind as regular and specific as the drum riffs Buzz devised.

Buzz returned with the band. He reconnected with Jab and Mark, and the late nights at the farmhouse, the discussions, and music resumed. The BeeStings played out their week, and on the late Sunday morning, after pancakes and coffee, Jab and Buzz headed back to the venue where the band was meeting for a quick run-through of the evening's set. Jab ran a few errands for Hank and then stopped in to listen to the band and check with Buzz to determine if anything else was required. The two of them sat down and discussed the coming schedule, the time for the return of the band. Dates determined, they sat and talked. Buzz turned to Jab.

"Listen, Jab, I know you seem settled here, but think about this. We're planning a longer trip next time. Going to expand and try out some clubs in Texas. We could use a real roadie, someone who knows how we work. Think about coming with us. Talk to Hank about leaving for a few months, and tag along with us. I can let you know details in a while. What do you think?"

Jab's still face did not expose his rapid heartbeat. He sat quietly thinking that this was the answer to the craving he was feeling, to the itchiness he detected. He looked at Buzz. "Maybe. Let me know the plans and a timeline. Texas? Yeah, maybe so. Might know someone there. There are some things to take care of here, but I think that could be a good move for me."

Buzz smiled and nodded. "Great. It's not all worked out yet, but I'll stay in touch and we'll talk. Listen, I'm going back to the motel with the guys and get some sleep before tonight. We plan on leaving right after the set. Tell Mark thanks again, and I'll see him next time." And Buzz pushed back his chair, got up, and walked towards the door.

Jab stood up and watched him. Then he glanced at the table and saw the sticks that Buzz had forgotten. "Hey!" he yelled, "You forgot these!", and he held the drumsticks up.

Buzz turned around and grinned. "Keep 'em," he yelled back, "I have plenty," and he pushed open The Watering Hole's door and walked into the sunshine.

Hank Fontaine

I gotta say, I miss Jab. He was a good guy. Helpful, knowledgeable, willing to do and learn. I'm hoping when he's done with the band and the Texas trip, he'll return. I had plans for him. Wanted to make him a bigger part of The Watering Hole. Maybe even eventually partial owner, although not sure he had the cash to do that. Anyway, hope to see him again. Strange character though.

I knew something was in his mind when he came to me and asked if Richie, the musician/bartender he had hired, could be trained to do his job. He said it would be good to have a backup, to have someone who understood the organization of the venue, who could plan and supervise the music acts and work with the bands and musicians. I said that was a good idea, but I figured there was something else going on. I knew Jab was one of those roamers, one of those men who, for whatever reason, couldn't settle, and he had been around this part of the state for a long time. We talked, Jab and me, about his travels and thoughts, and I knew that despite his friendship with Mark and his work at the repair shop, he wouldn't stay around. Too bad. I listened when he explained about his plans to travel with Buzz and the band. I told him I hoped he would return, but he didn't say much. Just that he'd see and would let me know. So, I wished him luck, told him to keep in touch, and had a long talk with Richie who turned out to be a good choice. Not as good as Jab, but Jab taught him carefully, and he listened. Anyway, Richie worked out.

Jab just appeared one day, as the building was being reworked and changed into the restaurant, bar, and music venue my partners and I envisioned. I put most of the money into this place, although I didn't have enough to do it all. I did know a few people who had some ready cash, and they were OK with the plans I had, as long as they got their money back and made a bit more. I've always been good at planning and creating, and over the years moved from doing small projects to some medium sized ones, and then to larger enterprises, and The Watering Hole was one of the large ones. Working out so far. Been lucky about most of the people I hired to work here. Of course, there's been a few flakes and would-be criminals and swindlers. There always are in a big project like this one, but I know how to take care of them. Jab wasn't one.

He just walked in one day and found me and asked if I needed additional help. Said he would do anything that was necessary, and he had a few skills. He seemed like an honest sort, and I pride myself on being able to size up people, so I put him to work carrying in equipment and working with the carpentry crews and then the electricians, and he knew what to do. I kept an eye on him. Always careful. Have to be. Especially with the union guys since Jab was an outsider, but once I saw what he was able to accomplish, I didn't hesitate to use him for a few jobs on the side. He was good and careful, and I was glad to save some money. I paid him cash. When there was time, I began to talk to him, to sound him out. He was a thinker, and honestly, sometimes I wondered at some of the stuff he said. Turns out he had a few good ideas for the place, and I listened to him because, well, I just liked him. Jab was unafraid to admit when his didn't know something or couldn't do something. He wanted to learn. He worked as a barback for a while when we didn't have one, cleaning, stocking, filling in ice, and watching the bartenders who had been hired. Most of the time he had a book with him and on breaks would read. A few times, on his lunchbreak, I saw him reading through the *Old Mr. Boston Official Bartender's Guide* we had placed behind the bar. The bar served mostly beers and shots but now and then someone would ask for a mixed drink of some kind, and Jab said he wanted to be prepared. Just in case. He was right. There were several times we were short in that department and he took over the bar. Did a decent job as far as I could tell. No complaints.

Jab did the same thing in the kitchen. He wasn't a trained chef, but watched and asked if he could help. Just like the bar, there were times the kitchen was short-staffed, and he worked there. I positioned him as sous chef and line cook and dishwasher. He did it all, and did a decent job there too. The guy surprised me. Like when he came up with the idea to advertise on those billboards along Route 156. I was not for that plan at first because it was costly, and we were just getting the place started. But Jab made some calls, and talked to some people, and looked into it. He came to me with a plan that was workable, and turns out, he was right. Those billboards brought in travelers and vacationers who were looking for a place to stop and a drink and a rest. For a while, I considered building onto the place and adding a small motel, but that seemed too much. Anyway, it would take away from the motels in and around the town, and we all worked together and tried not to take too much business from each other. Always the best route. Still, I have that idea in the back of my mind. Who knows?

Jab did have some strange ideas. He was a reader and got most of them from the books he was reading. We talked about a few of them, and he offered to loan me some of the books, but I didn't take them. Not much of a reader, and had little time to spend with that anyway. One of the ideas Jab told me about stuck with me. He told me about some of the stuff he read and that *it was important to find a meaning and purpose in life.* Those are the words he used. He said that money was not always the answer. Not the meaning or purpose. I listened to him and asked some questions, but I have to say, I didn't agree with that. Money helped me succeed, helped to put my kids through school and make my wives, all of them, happy. At least for a while. Another story.

Jab had weird ideas about money. I saw him use his own cash at times. One or two musicians were running low on money and Jab put them up at one of the motels when he saw they were sleeping in their car and washing up in the bathroom. Once, some kids traveling through didn't have much and I saw that they ordered and shared the cheapest thing on the menu: a grilled cheese. They drank water. Jab was walking through and talked to them. He had the waitress bring them more food. He paid for it and tipped the waitress. I know because she told me. There was one particular family in the area who were hard up, and I saw them around town. Jab seemed to know them. He would go over and speak to them and once, I watched as he paid for their groceries at the town's Piggly Wiggly. And those were the times I saw or learned about what he did. I bet there were more times and instances, but Jab never said anything about it. Anyway, I noticed. Strange character, that Jab. Good guy. Hope he returns.

3. Ten-Dollar Bill
Meri

...though we may speak different languages, if we are men of good will we shall have a great deal to say to each other, and beyond what is precisely communicable we can guess and sense a great deal about each other. At any rate let us try.

I didn't expect to see him, and when he walked into the bar where I was working, I was more than surprised. I was pleased. Jab had called two or three times, leaving messages with one of my roommates, but I didn't return the calls. I think I was waiting to see if he would really turn up. I believe I was testing him. When he walked into Hopper's, I was more gratified than I expected to be. Or wanted to be.

I left Mark's farmhouse in Waterville with Wendy and Jen partly because of Jab. I was beginning to feel more than a friendship for him, and my brain cautioned me that a relationship with him would not end well. None of my relationships had. It was best for both of us that I leave, and when the opportunity came, when Jab was gone back to the Chicago area to visit his family, I packed up and left. I promised Mark I would stay safe and would call once I got settled, and I did. That was a mistake because Jab answered the phone. I probably should not have called.

I left with Wendy and Jen and got along with both of them although Wendy always seemed a bit flighty. Jen and I shared sly side-glances when Wendy made some of her crazy suggestions such as stopping in Hot Springs and taking baths there or visiting some of the old cemeteries she claimed were haunted. The trip to Dallas took four days because she insisted on doing those things, but since the car was hers and her parents' credit card was used for the motels we slept in, we went along with her suggestions. I guess it was fun. She was traveling to her sister and brother-in-law's house at the southern end of Dallas, and when we got there, they were kind enough to let Jen and me stay in the room above their garage until we figured things out. Jen and I found another girl who needed some roommates, and we moved into the apartment with her which was just on the outskirts of Dallas and found work. I started working at Hopper's Bar, and Jen waitressed at a restaurant close to it. Most of the time, we would walk to our jobs together. Sometimes, when our shifts coincided, we'd walk back to the apartment with each other, looking at the various businesses and trying out a new BBQ place. When there was time, and Wendy was available, the three of us would ride around in Wendy's car looking at the sights. I didn't know what I was going to do or where I would end up, but I was young and free, and glad to be away from my dad and stepmother and her two bratty girls. I figured I could take care of myself. I always had.

It was early evening and my shift was almost over when Jab walked in. The after-work crowd was thinning out, and I was considering where I could get a quick bite to eat when I left. I was able to comp a daily meal at Hopper's, but wasn't sure I wanted another burger or dish of chili. I thought I might stop at Jen's restaurant and see how close she was to finishing up, and my mind was concerned with these thoughts while I wiped the bar and grabbed more Lone Stars for the couple seated in front of me. From the corner of my eye, I saw a familiar figure, but it wasn't until he sat down and I turned towards him that I realized it was Jab.

"Howdy, Meri," and he grinned as he saw the startled look on my face. "Glad to see you. How are you?"

"Jab! You did show up. I'm fine. Are you here with that band? How long are you staying?"

He started to talk, but a few more people sat down and I needed to get their orders, so I plopped a beer in front of him and said, "I'm off in about thirty minutes. Can you wait?"

He nodded, and I went to finish serving drinks. I spoke to Bill who was taking my place, finished up at the bar, and checked out for the day. I came around to the other side of the bar, stood next to him and suggested we leave and go somewhere to talk. We walked slowly down the street and came to a small diner where we went in and sat at a booth. After ordering, we settled back to catch up with each other's news. I knew about Jab's decision to travel with a band and listened as he told me about their plans.

"There are some gigs around here for the next ten days, and then we're traveling south towards Austin. Buzz scheduled some stops along the way. Then we'll go to Houston for a month or so then come on back up here. There are plans to travel west after that, but I'm unsure of where exactly that will be. Anyway, I have about an hour now before I need to get back to help set up. I told Buzz I was meeting a friend for a drink.

Tell me how you're doing. Do you like it here? Where are you living? Staying for a while?"

We finished eating and compared likes and dislikes about Texas. Jab said he hadn't been here long enough to form any real preferences and said he would hold his review for a while. The hour passed, and we made plans to meet in a couple of days when he'd have some time to come to Hopper's. We left the diner and walked to where he left his bike. I waved him off and went to Jen's restaurant where I waited for her to complete her shift.

The next time I saw Jab, he waited until my shift was over, and we took a table and sat in the back of Hopper's drinking and talking. When there was a lull in the conversation, Jab looked up and saw the dartboard which was just behind me. He grinned.

"Ever play darts?" he asked.

"A few times. This board rarely gets used," I answered.

"Let's play," he said, "and the loser buys dinner."

We got up and gathered the darts and took a few practice throws each before we started. I wasn't very good, but frankly Jab wasn't either, and we joked that we were perfectly matched. We played three rounds and decided that would be enough. We finished our drinks, I gathered my purse, and that night, Jab bought dinner.

For the following week or so, that's what we did. Jab would come in to Hopper's and wait for me while I finished my shift. We'd talk and play three rounds of darts, and then finish up at one of the restaurants in the area. We were evenly matched because after four of these *dart dates* (Jab named them.) we had each paid for a couple dinners. The last time we met was right before Jab was due to leave with the band and travel. He said they'd be gone for five to six weeks, and he'd call me to check in. I was sorry to see him leave but also relieved. I enjoyed being with him, and he never pressed me for more than a friendship, but I knew we were attracted to each other, and I didn't want to be. That night, when Jab left, we hugged good-bye. That's all.

Jab did call, and we spoke briefly each time. He said the traveling was both hectic and tiring, but he liked moving around and meeting different people and seeing various parts of Texas. We joked that because I had been practicing darts in his absence (I hadn't.) that I would beat him when he returned to the area. We made plans to see each other again. When he did come back, when he walked into Hopper's again, I was pleased to see him. And again, wished I wasn't.

This time the band played in bars around the area for almost three weeks. We continued seeing each other, playing darts, and having dinner. A few times, I took Jen with me, and once Wendy came, and we went to hear the band at whichever bar they were performing. I introduced them to Jab, and we met the band members, and a couple times, all of us hung out. There was nothing serious between Jab and me, but I knew he would welcome more than a friendship. I wasn't looking for that, at least not then, and I never encouraged anything. Sometimes I look back at that time and wonder if I should have. Regrets are regrettable.

It was our last dart date, and I had been on a roll and winning. As a joke, I said, "For this game, let's put some real money on the outcome. This time when I beat you, I'll have something to show for it. What do you think?"

"Sure. Think you will win? How much?"

I reached into my pocket and pulled out a bill. It was ten dollars.

"How about this?" and I waved the bill around.

Jab nodded and grinned. "Fine. Ten bucks it is." He took up his darts and rubbed them between his hands. "Let's go!"

We played. I'm not sure whether it was the act of betting actual money or just an arrogance on my part, but I lost that game. I played poorly, and when all three rounds went to Jab, I sighed. I took the bill from my pocket, went to the bar, and grabbed the first pen I saw. It was red, and across the bill I wrote *Won at Hopper's* and handed it to Jab. He read it and laughed.

"There you are," I explained, "and when you spend it, you'll remember my poor performance tonight!"

Jab took the bill, folded it into thirds and placed it into his wallet. "Won't be spending this one," he said, "no matter if it's my last bill. Going to keep it to remind me of tonight," and we smiled at each other.

The band was getting ready to leave again. This time they were headed to west Texas, towards Lubbock, or at least that was their plan. The last time I met with Jab, right before they left, he brought up the subject I'd been avoiding. He asked about my feelings towards him, and let me know what his were towards me. I felt bad because I couldn't, or didn't want to have more than a friendship. Not then.

"...and I feel awful telling you this," I continued, "but right now I don't want more than what we have. I'm not saying never, but I think that, for now, it's best to keep this a friendship. Can you understand, Jab?"

He looked at me and gave me that sideways smile he had. "Sure, Meri. I just wanted you to know how I felt. *We may speak different languages...but we can guess and sense a great deal about each other...*"

I looked at him. "What is that? What do you mean?"

Jab smiled again. "Just something from a book I read," he explained, "Something I think fits."

We spoke for a while longer, and then he had to leave. He said he would call when he could and check in again. I hugged him good-bye, and this time, I added a kiss on his cheek. He turned to walk to his bike, and I stood and watched him, just like the time in Waterville when I stood and saw him leave to visit his Chicago area family. I waved again, although I'm not sure he saw me. I waited until I could not see him or hear his bike. Then I turned and began to walk to my apartment.

***

Jab did call a few times, and we talked briefly. The last time we talked, he said he would not be returning with the band. He would not be coming back to the Dallas area. He and the band weren't that far from New Mexico, and Jab said he had a feeling he should travel there. He told Buzz his plans, and they parted friends. He said he would miss being with the band, but it was time to travel on. Jab said he was sure we would see each other again, and we needed to stay in touch. I agreed. Then he said some sweet things to me. Things meant only for me. Things I remember. Years later, when I saw him again, I reminded him about what he said. He told me he remembered, and we spoke about the sweetness.

4. Swiss Army Knife

Think of it... that in your heart there is an answer to all the things and sights of the world, that everything concerns you, that you ought to know as much about everything as it is possible for man to know.

Jab pulled open the nail file from the red handle of the knife and cleaned his nails as he leaned against the wooden building. He was on a break and was working to get the blue masa out from beneath his nails. The *adoolii* was tasty, and the tortillas made from it always sold quickly, and since they were a staple at the Dulce Café, he seemed to be forever working at cleaning his nails. He sighed, wiped the file on his jeans, and slipped the Swiss knife back into his pocket. He felt around in his shirt pocket for the packet of cigarettes and remembered he had stopped smoking some weeks ago. Bad habit. Expensive. He sighed again. He was tired from staying up too late again while talking to Mangas, the old man from whom he rented a room. The old man had so many stories to tell about the Jicarillo Apache tribe that he never seemed to repeat any. Jab was fascinated by the history and mythology Mangas told him, but he was sure the *tesquino*, the corn brew Mangas had just finished making and of which they had consumed quite a large amount last night, had something to do with his exhaustion. Not his fault. The tesquino needed to be consumed as soon as it was prepared or it would turn sour and be undrinkable. Jab hoped there wasn't much left for tonight.

He turned to go back into the kitchen and finish cleaning up. It was just after three o'clock, and there were few customers left. The café would close soon, opening again in the morning at six, but Jab needed to be in the kitchen at five, helping Ela to prepare the breakfasts that would be sold and make the sandwiches the men would purchase for their lunches or as a supplementary snack before they went to the oil and gas fields to work. Jab wiped the ancient wooden tortilla press, cleaned the flat top grill, and went out to wipe down the counters and the few tables before washing the floor. When he finished, he put the cleaning supplies away and went back to ask Ela if she needed anything else done.

"No, Jab. *Ahe`he`e.* You're a good worker, and I know you're tired. Don't let that old man keep you up tonight! And don't drink more of that tesquino. Kills the brain. That old man has none left," And Ela smiled as Jab laughed. Mangas was Ela's father. She said the same thing every time Mangas brewed the drink although she had a few sips herself last night.

"OK, Ela. I'll behave," and Jab left to walk to the rickety wooden cabin built a few dozen steps behind the café. He thought he'd try to get a short nap and maybe a quick shower, if the water was warm. Sometimes it wasn't.

***

The town of Dulce, New Mexico was important to the Jicarillo Apache tribe because it was the site of their tribal headquarters. The burgeoning gas and oil fields provided work for many of the men of the tribe. The town itself was expanding, and additional houses were being built and lining newly-created streets; business were popping up along the main thoroughfare through town, and the elementary school and high school were filling up with the children of the town's residents. Two yearly celebrations: the Little Beaver Celebration, and the Stone Lake Fiesta, were creating a public interest, growing in popularity, and bringing in tourists. People in town were mostly content. It was a pleasant life although a hard one. During the year or so Jab had lived in the town he had made friends and was pleased to live in an area which seemed so free and encouraged his respite.

Jab had settled in Dulce after a few years wandering around the southwestern part of the country. After his experience with the BeeStings and Buzz, he discovered he was needed back in the Chicago area where he spent a summer with Jan and his mother after his father's death. He didn't remain, and although he periodically called or dropped a postcard to what remained of his family, he continued his wandering. Sometimes he would stay in a place and find a job for a couple months and meet new people. He was always moving, always searching. He just wished he knew for what.

He spent most of a year in Albuquerque, New Mexico, staying at a cheap motel for a while and then moving to another, working a job as a mechanic and then as a short-order cook, and even for a brief time, as a bouncer at a club. He moved from place to place and job to job, and met new people, and picked up books along the way, reading and discussing novel ideas with whomever would talk to him. He discovered that the southwest area seemed slower to react to cultural changes, less interested in political policies, less attentive to radical reforms. A war had started in the Middle East, a new president had been elected, and climate changes began to creep into the south and the Pacific Northwest in the forms of killing heat and dangerous eruptions. But the quiet towns, the gentle life, the untroubled behaviors Jab encountered soothed his wired nature, eliminated the stress he discerned when he read a newspaper or, rarely, watched the television news. He could ignore the advertised ugliness as he rode his bike into the desert and gazed at the cacti, the desert willow, the pampas grass. The marginal, muted towns he traveled through on his rides offered wooden structures housing a fan, tendering a cold beer, providing a chance to meet with bydwellers and converse with them. He stopped and took advantage of ease, and listened, and learned, and discovered a connection with a group he had never known existed.

The Jicarillo Apache tribe underwent the usual hardships afforded the many indigenous groups in the United States. Battles were fought, land was overtaken, reorganization and nomadic existence was forced, and finally, after the last world war, much of the tribe was established in the northern area of New Mexico, near the Colorado border in a place which was not their traditional sacred lands, but was given to them as recompense. They settled. And, using the lawful methods learned from their overlords, they began a decades long legal battle to regain what was theirs. Jab connected with their story and began to seek them out, these native inhabitants with whom he had no blood connection but only a felt spiritual one.

When he tired of his own nomadic life, he spent some of his secreted money on a better motorcycle, one whose ability to travel far distances he trusted, searched out a map, and left for the tribal lands. He rode into Dulce, New Mexico where he met and quickly bonded with Ela and more slowly, with her father, Mangas, and learned that *Da anzho ash!* was a greeting to a friend and *Ahe`he`e* was a thank you. Ela's husband had died, leaving the running of their café to her and their son, Elan, who wanted to go to college and was not happy making the sandwiches, flattening the adoolii into tortillas, sweeping the floors, tasks that Jab was willing to undertake. So, he was hired by Ela, introduced to Mangas whose small wooden structure he shared, and invited to live in Dulce. Not as a member, but a treasured and trusted outsider.

***

The water was warm, and after a shower and brief nap in the heat of the day, Jab came out to the small kitchen and living area where Mangas was seated, listening to the radio, sipping a root beer. Jab nodded a greeting and began to mix and knead the dough for the fry bread they would eat later with the stew left from the night before.

The fry bread was a favorite with Mangas. The meal preparation was simple, the food tasty, and Jab was happy to take over the cooking for the two of them. Sometimes Ela joined them, bringing a soup she made containing summer squash, spinach and cornmeal dumplings, or food left from the café, food which was not traditional but could not be wasted. They would eat and discuss, and after clean-up, Ela would walk back to her small house one street away, and Jab and Mangas would spend the weekday nights talking.

It had taken some time, and Mangas needed to be won over, but his daughter, Ela, convinced him that this young man could be trusted. Jab promised Ela that he would help Mangas out when the offer of a room was made. The amount he would pay Mangas for being allowed to sleep in the small back bedroom, would be useful in helping to purchase the medicine from the town's only pharmacy which assisted in the regulation of Mangas' disease. An agreement was reached and hands were shaken. A man's word must be trusted. It took a while, but Mangas began to like this man who listened, who was attentive, who asked wise questions and offered salient comments as they spent the nights together, waiting out the setting of the sun, noticing the arrival of the stars and the moon. Mangas appreciated this person with the strange name, and during the last celebration, the Little Beaver Celebration, when Jab honored the tribe by attending and playing in the softball tournament, leading the Dulce team to a victory, Mangas honored Jab with the Swiss army knife he watched him use daily.

Mangas was a *warrior-chief.* True, there were many in the town, but he was one of the oldest and wisest, and was honored during various times of the year, especially at his birthday, with many small gifts. The Swiss army knife has been given to him several years ago by a family in the town who were no longer present, having moved south to take care of other family members. There was no dishonor in passing on an honored gift, and Mangas wanted to show his appreciation to this man, to Jab. He was pleased as he watched Jab handle the knife, use the small blade to slice open the envelopes received in the mail, twist the tiny screw driver to tighten the arm of Mangas' eyeglasses, engage the bottle opener to flip off the tops of the cold root beer they enjoyed. It was good to see the gift in use, to note gratefulness in this man as he carefully wiped the red cover and replaced the knife in his pocket. Jab honored the gift, and thus honored Mangas.

On weekends, when the sky remained light, they would travel the street to Ela's house, Mangas leaning on the strong arm of his companion. Upon arrival, Ela and Mangas would talk on the telephone to Elan who was away at school learning and becoming educated. Then neighbors would gather in the front of the house, and one or two additional warrior-chiefs would take seats on the porch next to Mangas, and the crowd would listen to the stories and the history of the tribe expounded upon by the chiefs. Drums would appear, and old songs would sound in the area, and small children would play in the back, dancing to the pulsing echoes of the instruments. Root beer and other libations would be passed around, and Jab would sit at the back or stand at the side and listen to the tales and store up questions he would ask Mangas afterwards as they walked back to the wooden building.

The tales would be didactic, often involving *Coyote*, who could be good or evil depending upon the tale. Coyote stole fire for man and was sometimes scheming and other times smart. There were tales of the Trickster Fox and Bobcat and Dragonfly, a creature Jab would encounter again in another place. The tale of the creation of the tribe was told many times, and each time, it seemed to Jab, told differently. He relished listening to these stories, hearing about the lands given by the Apache Creator, *Ussen*, about the four sacred rivers, and the mountains which both needed and gave protection. Jab learned where the name Jicarillo came from, that it means "little baskets" and refers to the drinking vessels he noticed the neighbors holding and from which they sipped their drinks. The little drinking baskets being held were not the only baskets made by the artisans of the tribe, and when Jab heard of his sister's wedding, he sought out and found two hand-woven, decorated baskets which became gifts for his sister and his mother. He was not at her celebration, and he regretted that. The patterned baskets were sent along with a short letter which included both his regret and his love.

The days and weeks and months passed. Jab was happy, and Mangas was content, and when the old warrior-chief became increasingly ill and there was no hope, Jab would return from his workday at the Dulce Café to the wooden building, and make the fry bread and encourage Mangas to eat some of it dipped into the gravy of the stew. And when the warrior-chief could only swallow small sips of water, when his voice faded away and he could no longer tell his tales and recount the history, Jab would raise a small drinking basket to the old warrior-chief's dry lips and repeat the tales he learned back to the man who listened and nodded slowly, the only movement he could create. When the warrior-chief was finally conclusively silenced, and the burial took place that same day in the ancient way, and Mangas' clothes and effects were burned, and his small wooden house was pulled down to ensure that no angry ghost would be present, Jab stood back and watched and mourned. And when Ela, who also followed the new Christian religion, had a church service dedicated to the remembrance of the warrior-chief, Jab attended, and the tears he shed were partly for Mangas, and partly for his own dead father, and partly for himself and the losses he felt, and partly for the ache he recognized but could not define. And now, after another winter had passed and the infancy of spring prevailed, Jab knew it was time to travel.

He made plans. He tuned up his bike and readied it for the journey. He packed his belongings and visited the burial place of Mangas, whispering to the warrior-chief for a final time, the tales he had learned from him. Then he returned to the house one street away from the café. He told Ela he was leaving and thanked her for housing him after the warrior-chief's wooden structure was pulled down. She listened attentively and understood.

"You will be missed, Jab. My father told me you were like the first son he and my mother lost before I was born. He said he saw someone's eyes through yours. He did not know whose they were, but hoped your eyes were the eyes of that child, of Tarak. He told me long ago that you would leave, that you are a wanderer, and I should not expect you to remain. You are always welcomed here. I will miss you," and Ela hugged him. "Return when you can. Safe journey."

Jab kissed her cheek and left the house. He checked his bike, secured his duffle bag to the back, and rechecked his pockets for the essentials: his wallet, his money, his Swiss army knife. He pulled his helmet on, turned the key, and slowed wended his way towards the main road. He wasn't sure where he would go, but it didn't matter. Before he turned onto the paved highway, he pivoted to the side of the dirt road and turned to look back at the town he had just left. He couldn't see the café, but he knew it was there; he knew Ela would be inside wiping the tables and cleaning the floor; he knew she would ready food for the next day; he knew she would grind the blue masa and prepare the tortillas using the ancient wooden press. He sat for some minutes thinking, wondering if he had learned as much as was possible for him to learn from this experience. He hoped he had. Turning once again to the road, he checked for traffic. There was none. He headed north.

Ela

I did not tell Jab what I knew, what my father had told me. Mangas knew he would come, and when he showed up at the café, I knew my father had been right. Here was the man who would help me and work in the kitchen while my son, Elan was away becoming educated. Here was the man who would help with my father and watch him while he finished this life. Here was the man who would be an outsider but would also join our town, understanding our ways, respecting our beliefs. I liked Jab right away, and while my father pretended to hesitate in accepting him, I knew it was his way, his habit. He had told me about Jab.

"There is someone who will be here to help you now that I no longer am able to," Mangas explained. "He will stay until I am gone and I will tell him the legends and make and share the *tesquino* with him. I will recognize his eyes. I am hoping it is my firstborn's eyes, your brother Tarak's eyes, I will see. You will know this man when he comes."

And it was Jab who came.

He was a good worker and a fast learner. And when I came to work early the morning after I hired him, and saw that he had made a bed for himself at the side of the building, keeping his motorcycle close to him, he did not sleep there another night. I took him to Mangas and the house and showed him the small bedroom he could rent, and Jab was glad. Mangas pretended, in his way, to hesitate in accepting Jab, but I knew he would. Jab would cook for him, and as I did the daily paperwork after the café was closed, I was glad to have that help. Mangas refused to move in with me at my house just a street away. He said he was more comfortable in the wooden structure even though I worried, afraid it would catch fire. My father told me that he was meant to spend his last days there, as warrior-chiefs in the past did, and I accepted his pronouncements. He came to my house each weekend, and the neighbors gathered, and we listened to the old men, the old warrior-chiefs, tell the histories and sing the songs and share the drinks. It was good to be together. Good to see my father, the best and oldest warrior-chief, gather the respect he deserved, the respect owed to him. It was good to have Jab there listening and talking to Mangas. He was accepted by my father which meant he was accepted by all.

Once I asked Mangas if Jab was indeed, Tarak, my older brother, if he had Tarak's eyes. My father looked to his right and then to his left, letting me know he was considering how to answer me. I waited.

"I am unsure," he finally said, "I think maybe not although I wish it was so. I would like to see my son grown and here with me, but there is something in the face of Jab, something which tells me another spirit resides. Perhaps Tarak. Perhaps not. This man, this Jab, is a wanderer, and whoever he is, I am glad he is here. My dreams told me he would come," and that is all my father said about the matter.

Jab was smart. I showed him how to make the tortillas using the blue masa and the ancient wooden press that was my great-grandmother's. I explained the kinds of sandwiches the men who went to the oil fields liked best and showed him how to wrap them in a special way so they would stay fresh for hours until they had time to eat them. I helped him when the cleaning was to be done, but after the first day, he said he could do it, and I should go back to the things I needed to finish. When I cooked at home, when I made the squash soup my father liked, I would bring it over to the old wooden structure, and we would share the meal. Jab grew expert at making the fry bread, almost better than me, and the three of us would sit and eat the evening meal, and Jab would open the root beer with the opener from his little red knife, and my father, as long as he was able, would tell the stories I remembered from my childhood. We were content. And on those times when my son, Elan, was able to come home for a time, the four of us were content, and I saw Mangas' face and thought he would live a longer life. I was sure the sickness he had would go away and allow him to remain. I did not want to lose him. My mother and my husband and my young daughter were gone. All too soon, and I wanted to keep Mangas, my father, the oldest warrior-chief of our tribe, here in the living world.

But the time came when Mangas was no longer helped by the medicine, and the doctor I insisted we go to took me to the side and told me to make him comfortable and gave me more medicine to ease the pain which would arrive. I saw Mangas grow weaker and quieter, and there was a time when he could no longer lean hard upon Jab's arms and walk to the house to tell the tales. The women and men of the tribe, a few families at a time, came to visit Mangas, came to pay their respects to my father, came to say their good-byes. And before he lost his voice, before he was not able to make his wishes known, my father, Mangas, called me to his bedside and told me what to do.

"You must follow the old ways when I go. I listened to you and your husband when your mother, my wife, died, and I have regretted it. Bury me before the day is out. Place my tribal clothes on me and put my important belongings with me. Tear down and burn this house. I will not return as an angry ghost if that is done. The other warrior-chiefs will tell you which prayers and songs should be offered. See them and listen to them. Do this, my daughter, and follow the old ways," and I saw that Mangas was exhausted after this pronouncement.

"I will do that, Father," I said, and kissed his cheek. I went to the other warrior-chiefs the next day and followed their directions.

When my father's spirit left, Jab helped me carry out the ceremonies. My son, Elan was not able to get home in time, and I was grateful to Jab for his assistance, for his reverence and respect to a way which was not his. I hoped he would stay, but I remembered the words Mangas told me, and when Jab came to me and said he would be leaving, I was saddened. But this was expected, and I understood. His is a wandering spirit, and my father had told me about his going just as he told me of his coming.

I watched him on that last day. I wished him luck and safety and told him he would always be welcomed back, although I knew he would never return. He had been staying with me for the months after Mangas' wooden house had been torn down, and I was grateful for his company, for his help, for his respect.

When he went from my house, I stood at the window and watched him. I saw him turn his motorcycle and drive through the town. As I watched Jab leave, I spoke aloud to my father, to Mangas, and asked him to watch over not only my son Elan, but this man too. This man who had helped me and lived with us and listened to the stories and tales of our people and appreciated the voice of my father. This man who had a wandering soul and might have been the spirit of my long-gone brother. This man who stayed with my father, Mangas, the tribe's warrior-chief, and made him the frybread he loved, and cared for him as a son would, and earned his trust. And when I could no longer see the man, I went to the café where I ground the blue masa and prepared the tortillas using my great-grandmother's ancient wooden press.

Fry Bread Recipe

Ingredients

All-Purpose flour	4 cups to start. More for mixing might be needed.
Baking Powder	2 tablespoons
Salt	1 teaspoon. More if salty taste is wanted.
Warm water	About 2 cups.

Oil for frying

Directions

* Mix dry ingredients.

* Add warm water about ¼ cup at a time.

* Knead about 5 minutes to form soft dough. Add additional flour as needed. Do not over knead or bread will be hard.

* Divide large ball of dough into about 8-10 smaller balls and roll in flour.

* Cover smaller balls and let rest about 1 hour.

* Heat oil in a pan until very hot.

* Take one ball of dough at a time, stretching it out into a round tortilla shape.

* Carefully place in hot oil until golden brown and then turn to other side. Bread will puff up. Do not over fry.

* Drain on towels.

* Serve with stew or beans.

5. Three Pens

Please, just before going to sleep look up for a while at these bays and straits again, with all their stars, and don't reject the ideas or dreams that come to you from them.

It didn't take long for Jab to realize that traveling straight north was a mistake. Parts of the road were closed due to the big snows which had not completely melted in the nascent spring, and the ruralness of the alternate byways was difficult on a motorcycle, so he backtracked, traveling south and then east, and when he arrived at Taos, he found a motel and slept. The next day, after several cups of coffee and a breakfast of bacon and eggs, he obtained a map of the area, and as he planned, he thought: *I should have done this before. I can't be in a hurry to go nowhere in particular.*

He took stock of his money. While he had spent little of his earnings from Dulce, he knew he would need to be careful. He would also need to find places to live and to work. This did not worry him. He was resourceful and enterprising. There was no work he would disdain, no job he would scorn. He had worked in restaurants and bars and as a mechanic. He had delivered food and worked as a farmhand. It was all honorable, and he would do what was necessary, accepting the experiences and learning from them. Once again, he inspected the motorcycle, realizing it was receiving constant use and would not last forever, organized his meager store of personal effects, and began his journey. He drove to Interstate 25, finished traveling through New Mexico, and crossed over into Colorado, stopping when he was tired and it was dark. He traveled through towns noted on the map, through Trinidad and Colorado Springs and into Denver where he stayed for a time. He found small motels where he could rest and shower and think. There were some times, between the map-noted towns, when no affordable motels were available, and some of those dark nights were spent sleeping in out-of-the-way small spaces or in a rest area, his bike pulled over to protect and as protection. He planned on staying for a time in Denver where he was sure there would be opportunities and a bed for him.

There were. He washed dishes at a small restaurant where he was paid daily in cash. After a week or so, he was able to secure a motel room and was grateful for the hot shower and semi-soft bed. He stayed for a time, working first as a dishwasher, and when his culinary talent was discovered, as a fry cook. He worked any shift he was needed, and slept when he wasn't working, and saved his money. Having given up smoking except for the few times a cigarette was offered to him, and taking advantage of his comped meal at the restaurant allowed him to squirrel away needed cash.

Jab got along with the other workers. He was affable and civil although he kept to himself. When a shift was over and he was invited to join the other cooks and servers for a beer, he sometimes accompanied them, but he never stayed long. He finished a beer, excused himself as being tired, which was the truth, and would find his way back to the motel, taking a shower and reading some book he had picked up at a thrift-store before laying on the bed and sleeping until time for the next shift. He kept this up for a month or so before pulling out the map to plan where he would travel next. And one morning, he packed his duffle bag, checked out of the motel, and not bothering to give notice to the restaurant, inspected his bike, pulled on his helmet, and left.

He crossed over the next state line to Wyoming. He continued riding on I-25, eventually switching to I-90, and continued to travel north. He would ride and stop and sleep and eat and ride and stop and sleep and eat. He eased the bike through the roads and streets as he traveled through the towns, small and large, map-noted and not. Cheyenne, Casper, Buffalo, and finally, Sheridan, where he stopped for a longer time. He stayed because he had a feeling. He paid attention to his feelings, to his dreams. He found another small restaurant needing another transient cook, and he made another temporary home in another cheap motel and began to listen to others talk and look for another, different opportunity.

On his hours off, Jab visited the used car lots in the area, searching through the offerings for a different vehicle. *Maybe a truck,* he thought. *I know how to take care of those. Did plenty at Mark's place.* The salesmen got used to seeing him and answered his questions and marked him as just someone who was a looker and not a buyer. After a while, he was ignored. Meanwhile, he saved every cent he could, worked all the shifts he was offered, and bought nothing except for the ten-cent old paperbacks he found at the thrift stores he visited. He even denied himself the occasional beer with fellow workers who, after the first couple times of being turned down, no longer asked him to join them. He scrimped and worked and had a bit more than three hundred dollars saved. Of course, that was everything. Once he spent that he could afford to buy nothing. Not another week at the motel. Not another ten-cent paperback at the thrift store. The only thing to do was to trade-in his motorcycle, buy the five-year old pick-up truck, and hope for the best.

"Got a great buy there," said the only salesman who would actually talk with him. The salesman was young and new and anxious, and let the truck go for less than he should have. He regretted it later in the day, when he would be screamed at for an hour by his boss who saw Jab drive off the lot with the full tank of gas that was gifted to him.

Jab knew what he had planned. He had listened to the talk and read the local paper and discovered a nearby ranch, a century old one, a former cattle ranch which currently maintained horse stock and was looking for help. The Elston Ranch was about fifteen miles west of Sheridan and was a popular vacation destination for families and *drugstore-cowboys*, as some of the townspeople called them. Of course, the townspeople were polite to their faces when the visitors were in town and happy to see them spend their money in the shops and businesses which relied, at least partly, on their presence. Jab had ridden his motorcycle out to the area some days ago, found the ranch and its manager, completed a form which outlined his abilities and work history, and was hired as an assistant cook with decent pay, lodging and meals included. On the day Jab drove off the used car lot with his newly-purchased truck, he had already checked out of the motel, quit his restaurant job, packed his duffle bag, and left with two dollars and eighteen cents in his pocket. There was a ten-dollar bill tucked away in his wallet, but that wasn't for spending.

Elston Ranch was located on thousands of acres, in a valley against the Bighorn Mountains in northeastern Wyoming. While it was open for business year-round, the busiest time for the ranch was early spring to late fall, during the months vacationers would flock to the ranch to enjoy the plains and the mountains, to walk in the wooded areas and fish in the streams and creeks, to ride the horses and swim in the pool, to take in the scenery and snap photographs of the family, all wearing cowboy hats and red kerchiefs, hoping one would be good enough to turn into a Christmas card. The ranch was well run and the owners prided themselves on the quality and quantity of activities, entertainment, and recreation provided. And the meals offered were considered top-notch.

Jab pulled his truck into a parking space and entered the main hall where he was greeted by a young man who, once discovering who and what he was, advised him where he was to park and where he should enter. Not through the main doors. That was for guests. Jab nodded, went back to the truck, moved it to the appropriate lot, and went back to the large main kitchen where he found the head chef, Charlie Harper, and introduced himself. Charlie was a gregariously gabby middle-aged man who had run the kitchens at the ranch for a dozen years. His wife, Jess, was head of housekeeping, and they were content to live on the ranch through most of the year, visiting their grown son and his family in Montana each Christmas season, staying for a few months and spoiling their grandchildren. He shook Jab's hand, welcomed him into the kitchen and gave him a tour of the large area, annotating everything with more information than Jab could take in.

"…and in here are the uniforms. Come on down each morning… we start at six…and change into one of these t-shirts and some chef pants. After work, change and put your kitchen clothes over there on the pile for housekeeping. They'll get the clothes each day and clean 'em and put 'em back for us. Oh…and keep your hair short or pulled back, and that beard trimmed close. Don't want hair in the food. Speaking of which," and he pointed to a stack of large black-bound binders, "there are four of these *Kitchen Scriptures,* as I call 'em, that contain all the recipes we use as well as additional useful information. If you have any specialties, let me know. Always lookin' for different recipes to add to it. The one cook, Sam, is great at baking and Phil is real handy at butchering the meat. By the way, they came in yesterday and are out with the food truck getting some supplies so they should be back soon. You'll meet 'em then. Here, try this…" and Charlie reached into a large plastic container and grabbed two huge cookies. He gave one to Jab and bit into the other one.

Jab took a bite and nodded. "There are tasty," he said as he chewed, "From the *Kitchen Scripture?*"

Charlie finished the cookie before he answered, "Sam brought in the recipe and made them yesterday. She created it. Think we'll call them *Cowpoke Cookies* and the kids will love 'em. We get mostly families here. They check-in on Monday afternoon and stay until Saturday. After Saturday brunch, they depart, and we deep-clean, set things up, meet, plan for the next group. And staff has some time off until Sunday late afternoon when we prep for the week. We work long hours and work hard, but mostly get along, and it's a good place to be and enjoy this country. Take advantage of what's offered here, Jab. Most afternoons you have at least two hours free. Ever ride?"

Jab swallowed the last cookie bites and brushed off his hands. "Horses? Nope. Never have."

"Well, try it. The wranglers here are good, and they'll help you learn. Nothing like taking one of the trails with a horse and viewing the sights. Clears the mind and soothes the soul. Got a bag? Go get it and I'll take you to the room you'll share with Phil and a couple of the kitchen staff."

Jab went back to the truck to get his things, and when he returned, Charlie was taking to an older man who was lifting bags of potatoes and onions from a truck. He put his duffle bag and the two paper bags from his truck inside the kitchen door and went out to meet Phil and help carry in the supplies.

"Sam is here too, but…oh there you are," said Charlie, "Come over and meet the new addition," and he motioned to the person who was storing the bags inside the cavernous storage room.

Samantha Brainard walked over and held out her hand to Jab. "Hi, she said, "I'm Sam. Glad to meet you."

Jab smiled at the woman and shook her hand. "Jonathan," he said, "but I'm called *Jab*. Glad to be here." Introductions made, the four of them finished unloading the truck, placing the foodstuffs where they belonged, and then Phil walked out to move the truck.

"Come on, Jab. I'll show you to your room and explain the rules, and let you get settled. You have an hour or so, and then we need to get started with dinner. Lots of people to feed tonight even though no guests arrive until Monday. The whole staff will meet and eat in the guest dining room later. The wranglers and farmhands have their own kitchen area back by their sleeping quarters. There are two additional cooks who run that, and you'll meet them later. I oversee both kitchens." Charlie reached out to the desk that was next to the doorway and grabbed some forest green pens from the holder. He handed them to Jab saying, "Here. Always keep some of these on you. We write down everything…stuff we need, recipe changes, dates on food items…so keep 'em. Careful with these. Ordered cheap this year, and the gold print comes off. Wash your hands after using. No gold flecks in the food! Hey, grab some towels and sheets for yourself and here's your room…" and Charlie continued talking and pointing out the bed Jab would have and the communal bathrooms, and a million other things. Jab listened. He was quiet and content to begin his new venture.

***

Jab, with deliberate and measured control, pulled back on the reins and stopped his horse next to Sam's. They sat in the saddles, looking up at the Bighorn Mountains, taking in the majesty of the scene, breathing in the raw, pure air, and allowing the surroundings to energize them.

"Never gets tiring, does it?"

Jab smiled as he looked over to Sam, then leaned down to pat Cassie as she shook her head to disperse a fly. The mare whinnied softly as Jab continued to stroke her side. "Not for me, it doesn't," he answered, "Keeps me at ease."

Jab and Sam had gotten into the habit of riding through one of the Elston Ranch horse trails a couple times each week during their afternoon break. Sam had taken Jab over to meet her friend, Paul, one of the wranglers on the ranch, and Paul encouraged him to try riding.

"Nothing better," he explained, "and Cassie here is one of the best to learn on. She knows the trails, and enjoys them as much as the riders do. Come on, Jab, no sense living on a ranch and not taking advantage of the perks."

Paul was patient in teaching Jab how to approach and befriend the horse, how to mount and sit and steer the animal. He watched as Jab put the saddle pad and the saddle on the horse's back, as he tightened the girth and unrolled the stirrups, as he closed his fingers around the shortened reins. After the first few times around the corral, Paul called Jab a *natural* and praised his posture and confident manner. Jab visited Cassie on his afternoon breaks the remainder of the week, bringing her a vegetable treat from the kitchen and practiced saddling and mounting as Paul watched him ride in circles around the corral, periodically yelling suggestions. The following week, after Paul was satisfied that Cassie would be safe, Jab and Sam began their afternoon rides.

Working in the kitchen, despite the long, hot hours, was a pleasure for Jab. He enjoyed the variety of making new recipes, was learning to bake from Sam, and laughed heartily at the stories Phil would tell. They three of them got along, and once Phil realized Jab wasn't going to refuse to do any of the tasks he was given, the initial iciness which emanated from him melted. Now, a few months into the depths of the ranch's season, when the guest cabins were almost at full capacity and the entire staff worked even longer hours, the kitchen staff and the cooks worked like a well-oiled machine. They accepted that longer hours were required, and the leisure time allotted to them was prized. Jab and Sam continued their trail rides, allowing time with nature and the animals to refresh their spirits, to galvanize their mood. And they became friendly.

Walks to the horse barns and twice-weekly rides along the trails allowed Jab and Sam time and space to share personal confidences. Sam was a divorced mother whose ten-year old daughter lived with her parents in an apartment complex just south of Sheridan. She had worked at Elston Ranch for three years because it offered better pay than the bakery in town which was where she learned her baking competencies. She stayed with her parents and daughter every Saturday and Sunday when the workers were given their weekends off, and she visited at least once during the week so that she could spend time with Anna, her daughter, and tuck her in at night.

"That must be difficult, as a mother, not to see your child every day," Jab said.

"It is, but the money I make here really helps to provide for her. Helps my parents too. Dad is still working, but Mom isn't well and is a full-time grandmother. And you do what is necessary in life. You know that."

Jab nodded. "Still, ever think about going back to work at the bakery just to be near to Anna? Traveling back and forth must take a toll on you."

Sam shrugged. "Round-trip is less than an hour, and the ranch manager and Charlie are both understanding. I appreciate that. I do work part-time at the bakery during the winter months, but the pay is poor. Hoping to continue working here. Thinking that when Anna is older, she can get a job here during the summers. That would be great. She's a good kid, and I lucked out with her. She's smart, good in school, likes to read, and doesn't get into trouble."

They reined the horses over to the edge of the trail where a large gap through the brush and trees allowed them a different view of the mountains. Jab reached down to pat Cassie, looking ahead at the uppermost tip of the rocks where the clouds moved casually against the azure firmament creating artistic splashes. They watched for a time, talking silenced, welcoming the vision, lost in separate considerations and contemplations.

Jab spoke, breaking the quiet. "Look to the right. Think there are storm clouds coming. Not so sure the campfire will be held tonight."

"Well, the guides have alternate indoor plans: movies, or team games, or even a square dance which can substitute. Guess we should head back now. If they are inside, the kitchen will be expected to provide treats. No campfire roasts tonight," and she turned her horse around. They headed back.

"You don't have children, right? You've never said."

"No. Not yet anyway."

"Not yet? Planning on it? You've never said much about a girlfriend. Have someone special?"

Jab glanced at Sam and shrugged. "I thought so once, but we fell out of touch. Haven't spoken to her in over a year now. Not sure where she is."

Sam nodded. "Maybe you should find out. It's important to keep in touch with people. Maybe she's someone important to you, to your future. Could be she's waiting to hear from you."

"Could be," and Jab fell silent thinking about not being in touch. Thinking about Meri. Thinking about his sister and his mother. He had been dreaming about them lately. A feeling washed over him, something he wasn't expecting. A homesickness of sorts. He considered what he would do once this ranch season was over. Where he would go. Who he would see.

***

The season ended, and the last of the guests left. The kitchen crew was finished with the deep cleaning and storing away, necessary tasks in preparation for the following season. The wrangler kitchen would continue to be used, and Jab had helped Phil move leftover foodstuffs there. Elston Ranch never completely closed. An abbreviated kitchen staff, which included Phil, worked with the farmhands and wranglers who stayed and lived year-round at the ranch, caring for the animals and horses, watching after the many buildings, forming a family of sorts. Most of the staff was gone, and soon, Jab would commence his travels. He was in his quarters where he finished showering, dressing, and packing his duffle bag.

He and Sam had said their good-byes and exchanged whatever information they thought necessary earlier in the day. Sam was anxious to get to her parents' house and see Anna. She gave Jab the phone number and address of the apartment, telling him that there would always be an open couch waiting for him, should he choose to visit. Jab walked her to her car, carrying her bags, and they hugged before she got in and drove off.

"Listen, Jab, I sense you aren't the sort to stay in touch, but please do. Let me hear from you and know you are OK. You know, there is always a place for you here next season. Charlie likes you, and even that old grouch, Phil, seemed to. Maybe you could return next season?"

Jab smiled as he placed her bags into the back seat. Then he shut the door and turned to her. "Maybe. But if I'm being honest, it's not likely. I took to this place. Learned from being here, and will take those skills with me, but honestly, I'm ready to move on. Not sure where I'll go next. Maybe South Dakota. Might even get back to the Chicago area and see my sister and mother. Been a while for that. Might even try and get in touch with Meri too. Just don't know."

Sam looked up at him. "OK, Jab. Take care of yourself. Be safe. And I would appreciate you letting me know when you've landed somewhere. OK?"

"OK, Sam. Drive safely," and Jab accepted another hug from her.

He watched and waved as Sam pulled out of the lot and turned onto the main road to travel back to Sheridan and Anna. He went back to the kitchen and opened the door looking for the carrots he had stashed away earlier. With the vegetables in hand, Jab took a last walk to the horse stables, and when he saw Paul, he shook his hand and spoke his farewells. Then he went into Cassie's stall and gave the mare her good-bye treat. He patted her side and rubbed between her eyes and whispered a word of thanks to her. He stood for a bit and watched over the trails which led to the mountains. He would miss them. He turned and walked back to the emptying buildings, waving at the departing workers, stopping periodically to say something to one person or another, and finally reached his quarters.

He was the last one out of his room. All the roommates had left earlier, and Jab wanted to get on the road before it got too dark. He checked around to ensure nothing was left and picked up his jacket. Something fell out of the pocket and when he bent over to see what it was, a pen was on the floor. He checked the other pocket in the jacket where two more pens were discovered. Unzipping the duffle bag, Jab took the three forest-green pens with the flaking gold lettering, flipped them into the bottom of his bag, gathered his jacket, and turning out the light in the room, walked out of the building to his truck and got in.

Charlie Harper

When my wife, Jess, and I started at the ranch, we did it for a lark. We were tired of the daily grind, and not yet old enough to completely retire, so we took a chance and sold our house and most of our belongings and began working at Elston. We chose this ranch because it wasn't that far from our son's place in Montana, and boy, the beauty of this place! Jess and I always loved the outdoors and did a lot of camping, and this was sure a step up from the camping trips we took with our son when he was young. But we are happy being here and there's good people working here, and it's a great place to be most of the year. We've become friends with the year-round people, and have taken to the seasonal ones who come and work. Some of them are college kids, and they pretty much stick to themselves, but some of the older ones are interesting to get to know. Jab was one of those.

I mention Jab because he sticks in my mind. In some ways he reminded me of my son. About the same age, well younger, perhaps. But a decent fellow and hard worker. Had some interesting thoughts and I enjoyed our talks. Told him he was welcomed back for the next season. Even offered him a spot as a year-rounder helping in the wrangler kitchen. I thought it would be a good offer to Jab who seems a bit aimless to me. Phil is the main cook there during the off season and the winter, and I saw that the two of them got along. And that's saying something! I noted that over the season, Phil took a shine to Jab and got to trust him. Phil is an older guy, hardened by life and work and weather, and he's sometimes difficult to get to know. Took me a while. Sam took a shine to Jab too, and I was worried for a while. Ranch romances don't always turn out well, and I didn't want to see either of them hurt. But I was jumping the gun. From what I could tell, the two of them, Jab and Sam, were only just friends, and that was good. Better, in fact. I've seen some messes over the years.

Jab was real quiet at first. He knew his way around a kitchen, and was fast and accurate with the recipes. He wanted to learn; you could see that. He dug right in and did the grunt work Phil gave him to test him out and see if he was a slacker. But he wasn't, and did the peeling and cutting and measuring and mixing and carrying and cleaning, and didn't complain about it at all. Phil runs the guest kitchen when I'm busy at the wrangler kitchen, or in meetings, or doing the paperwork which was a pain, but required. He told me he gave those jobs to Jab to test him out and that he did OK, so Phil was happy with the turnout. Jab watched Phil and asked about some of his butchering techniques and did the same for Sam and her baking, so he was anxious to increase his abilities. He taught us something too. Jab brought a great fry bread recipe with him, and we used it all season. Asked him where he got it, and he just said, "Oh, just along the way." That was the way he talked, not giving up much about him or his past. And I let it go. Don't dig into what is not offered. Anyway, it was a good season, and if Jab doesn't come back next one, I know I'll miss him. Believe Sam will too. And probably Phil will. Hard to tell sometimes.

Strange thing about Jab. He became friends of a sort with Sam, and friendly with Phil and me, but there was something about him I couldn't figure out. Usually with the one-seasoners (that's what those people who come to work for a season and don't come back are called), they are running from something or hiding out, and they stay to themselves. Sometimes they are drinkers or, rarely, druggies, and we sort them out soon enough. Let them go. Try to be kind about it, but don't need them around when there are families with kids. Jab didn't appear to be in this category. He wasn't looking for a yearly job, and I couldn't tell that he was hiding anything, but I just couldn't get him. He was a strange fellow in ways. He wasn't unfriendly. In fact, most everyone liked him. He talked to people and always has something interesting to add to the conversation. He helped if someone needed something done and even joined in the poker games when one was organized. Good player too. I lost a few bucks to him.

I was talking with Jess about this and she asked, "What difference does it make as to the kind of person he is? You don't need to pigeonhole everyone. Let him be." Of course, she was right, but I liked to give identities to those I worked with. Phil was the *grumpy but dedicated old man.* Sam was the *hard-working single mother.* Even Jess had a phrase. She was the *smart-aleck wife with the handsome husband.* (I joke, of course. But not about the smart-aleck part.) I labeled others in my head, and would entertain Jess with my descriptions. But Jab… he was a strange knockabout. Wait…maybe *a strange knockabout* is the phrase? No. Still doesn't get to the heart of him. Can't pin-point Jab. Maybe I just don't know enough about him, and if he doesn't come back next season, well, that's that.

Anyway, this has been one of the best seasons for the kitchen. The crew worked together and got along. That has not always been the case. And that makes it easier for me. Don't know what will happen next season. I know Phil will be around, and Sam will return. Guess I'll just have to wait and see who applies for the other position. But I think I'll go to the main office and tell Nancy that if Jonathan/Jab Boyd applies again, he gets the job. No sense in looking for or training another chef if he wants the position. Strange or not, he's the one. One more year and I should figure him out. I'll give it some thought this winter when Jess and I are with the family. Certainly looking forward to that. Seeing my son and his wife and the kids makes it all worth it. Should be a great time. Always is.

Sam's Cowpoke Cookies

Ingredients

3 cups all-purpose flour
½ teaspoon salt
¾ cup light-brown or dark-brown sugar
½ cup white sugar
2 eggs
1 cup softened butter
2 teaspoon vanilla

Stir in 1½ cups of any of the following. Choose any three.
½ cup each of:
Chips: Chocolate, peanut butter, or butterscotch
Dried fruits: Raisins, cherries, or cranberries
Nuts: Pecan, walnut, or almond pieces
Shredded coconut
Small candies: M&M's, toffee bits, or Reese's Pieces

Directions

*Sift together dry ingredients (flour, salt, sugars).

*In a separate bowl, cream eggs, softened butter, and vanilla.

*Add wet ingredients to dry and mix.

*Stir in desired add-ins.

* Scoop dough with large cookie scoop and place on cookie sheet.

*Bake 350 degrees for 13-15 minutes until lightly browned. Cool.

Makes 12-15 large cookies.

Recipe can be doubled and tripled.

6. Beaded Keychain

Every important cultural gesture comes down to a morality, a model for human behavior concentrated into a gesture.

"…of course we named him at birth. His birth name is William, William Howe, but we are given various spirit names throughout life, to indicate a change in our situation or experiences. It is the Lakota way. William was a difficult birth for Mina, and we were worried about them both. Especially William. His first month was spent in the hospital, and we were all concerned. Now he is over a year old, is healthy and happy, and playing with his brother and sisters, so he gets a spirit name to honor that change. The ceremony will be at my cousin Tommy's farm next Saturday. He and Donna are hosting, and we want you to be there. Pass me that ketchup. Thanks," and Chaska poured the condiment over his potatoes. He and Jab were eating a late breakfast at the Pine Ridge Diner.

Jab swallowed the reminder of his coffee. "I would be happy to be there. Are you expecting many people?"

Chaska took a bite on his toast and answered, "Well, between Mina's family and mine and the elders of the tribe and some friends, maybe about a hundred. It is opened to all who wish to come, but I know many will be busy on a Saturday at noon. That's one of the reasons Tommy will have it there. You've been to his farm and know the size of it. There will be plenty of space if more people show up, and some will although it will be later in the day."

Jab took the last bite of his breakfast and pushed the plate away. He nodded when Pat, the waitress, held up the coffee pot, and mouthed *Thanks* when she refilled his cup. He turned to Chaska and asked another question.

"What will William's spirit name be? Did you choose it yet?"

"We do not choose spirit names. We won't know it until the end of the ceremony when *Wicasa Wakan*, you would call him a medicine man or holy man, explains what the name will be and why he will be given that name."

"So he picks it?"

"Yes and no. Mina's father, Takoda, is a tribal elder and lives with us. He has seen the change in William's health, has noticed his growth and happiness, and the name will come to him in a dream or a vision. He will meet with some other elders and the Wicasa Wakan, and together they will decide," and Chaska turned to Jab and smiled. "I suppose this sounds strange to you, how we do things, but it is our way, our tradition, and is important to us."

Jab shook his head. "No, not strange. I admire your culture and hope to learn about it, to learn from it. Your gestures are admirable, and I look forward to the ceremony. Should I bring anything? How should I dress?"

Chaska smiled. "Your presence is an honor, and dress comfortably. It is summer and will be warm, and we will be dressed in our best traditional clothes. Be at ease, my friend. Are we done here? We need to get back to the garage and see what we can do with that truck of Ray's." They waved to Pat and left to walk the two streets to Chaska's garage.

Jab met Chaska in much the same way he met Mark: in a bar drinking a beer and talking about old trucks and cars. Jab had been traveling for some months, stopping periodically to rest, to find a temporary job, once to nurse himself back to heath after catching a bad cold which turned into a fever and a hacking cough. Part of the winter months were spent in a small motel where Christmas was a bleak time spent thinking about his mother and his sister and wondering about Meri. He had spoken briefly to her roommate who told him that Meri left Texas and was moving to Tennessee to be with a cousin. Jab had a phone number for her there but had not called. Once he was back on the road, traveling east into South Dakota, he stopped in Pine Ridge which provided a cheap motel to stay for a time. It was a poor town. A quiet town. A town where people suffered and were brought close because of it. A town with understated honor. Then he met Chaska.

Chaska owned a garage in Pine Ridge, just off Main Street, close to Eagle Road. His business barely brought in enough to support his growing family, but he worked hard at it and was respected, and people trusted his ability and knowledge. He managed. Jab spoke to him, offering his services as mechanic, and Chaska agreed. The town, despite the difficulties and poverty, was pleasant and kind enough to house an outsider like Jab for a while, and Chaska offered the miniscule apartment just above the garage to Jab in return for his care of the place and his help with the cars and trucks which needed repairs,

"Keep an eye out for this place," suggested Chaska, "and we'll get along. Can't pay much, but will give you what I can, and I can use your help," and they came to an agreement.

The two men walked along the street, Chaska waving to other residents and business owners along the way, talking about what they might do to the old truck waiting for them. They entered the garage, lifted the wide door to allow in some air, and Chaska got into the truck and tried to start it. Nothing happened. He turned the key and held it. Nothing. Then he did it once more.

"Better stop," yelled Jab, "Come here and see what's going on," and Chaska climbed out and came over to Jab who was standing in front of the truck, hood lifted. Together they examined the truck's innards, pointing and playing around with a few things before standing back. Chaska took the rag from his back pocket and wiping his hands, he shook his head.

"Not so sure Ray's old truck will start this time. He has been bringing it here for me to work on for years now, and I've tried to care for it, but I told him a few months ago he needed to start searching for a replacement. Let's think about what else we can do, but if nothing works, I'll call him in the next few days with the bad news."

Jab nodded. "He sure is fond of this old heap. He babies it too. Guess it's headed for the junkpile."

Chaska looked at Jab. "The truck belonged to his youngest son. The one that was a Marine. He was killed in that suicide bombing in Beirut, and Ray never got over it. No junkpile. My bet is that it's placed in Ray's yard. And stays there," and Chaska sighed. "Well, I got one or two more things up my sleeve, and then we'll call it quits. Let me see what I can do with this."

Ray was a friend of Chaska's family, and was an elder of the tribe along with Takoda, Chaska's father-in-law. The two older men would spend many nights together, talking and sitting outside Chaska's yard under one of the chokecherry trees. Jab had become friendly with Takoda, and spent time listening and talking to him in much the same way he had with Mangas. Sometimes Jab would sit with Takoda and Ray, listening to their discussions about the famous tribal leaders, hearing the stories of Sitting Bull and Crazy Horse and Spotted Tail; of their visions and prophecies; of their exploits and adventures; of their hopes and dreams for the Great Sioux nation of which the Oglala Lakota are part. At times, the elders would begin to speak to each other in the ancient Lakota language, and then Jab would excuse himself, understanding that they wished to be alone but their value of politeness and kind etiquette did not allow them to ask him to leave. Jab would wish them a good evening and wander back to his small apartment where he would pick up a book and read until *han hay pee,* the night, brought its darkness.

***

Jab walked into the general store and began to look around for an appropriate gift. The baby, William, was just over a year old and he was at a loss to find something for the child. He wasn't even sure if bringing a gift was the proper thing to do, but he continued examining items, picking up various toys and clothes, looking at them and replacing them. A woman was behind the main counter, waiting on a customer, and when the transaction was finished, he smiled at her and asked, "Could you help me?"

"Sure. What are you looking for?"

"A gift for a baby. He's just over a year, and is having a naming ceremony. Not sure what is appropriate."

The woman thought and then asked, "Do you know his size? We have many cute outfits."

Jab shook his head. "I have no idea. Would that be appropriate?"

"I think it would. What about a stuffed toy? Or a baby game?"

"Well, there are other kids in the house, and I am sure there are lots of toys there. At least it seems like it when I've been there. What about a game for all the kids? I think their ages are nine, seven and five."

The woman walked around the counter and went to the sports section, and Jab followed. She picked up a stickball set containing two sticks and a leather ball. She grinned and said, "I played this when I was young, and it's a popular game around here. This is a sturdy set, and it will last until the baby is old enough to use it, but the other kids can use it now. What do you think?"

Jab reached out for the equipment and examined it. He nodded. "Do you have another set? That way each one will have a stick."

Another set was found. "Great. Can you hold those for me? Now I need a new shirt. Where would that be?"

He was shown the correct department and searched through the offerings until he found something suitable, and not too expensive, to wear. This was new to Jab who for years had bought his clothes at a second-hand store, but he was feeling generous. As he walked back to the front of the store to pay for his purchases, he passed the jewelry counter, and he stopped. He peered at the array of bracelets and necklaces, many of them sporting turquoise stones in various shades of blues and greens. But what caught his eye was a small, delicate silver necklace upon which hung a graceful silver dragonfly. Jab stared at the necklace until the woman who helped him came over and asked, "Do you want to see something?"

Jab pointed to the silver necklace. She opened the cabinet, reached in, and removed the item. She handed it to him and said, "That's a lovely thing. It's created by one of the Lakota artists from the Rosebud Reservation. The dragonfly stands for change and renewal. I have one tattooed on my arm. Look…" and she pulled up the arm of her sweater where a small blue dragonfly was stamped.

Jab admired it and smiling said, "That's a great tattoo. I never thought of getting one." He held up the silver necklace to the light and watched as the metal dragonfly danced in the brightness. He considered the gift and thought of his sister. "I'll take this necklace too. Thanks for your help."

She carefully removed the necklace from his outstretched hand, and placed it in a small plastic container. They went to the counter where Jab paid for the purchases and watched as they were carefully wrapped. He thanked her again, took his packages, and, feeling content, walked back to the small apartment just above Chaska's garage.

***

Jab stood to the side where he had a view of the proceedings. There was a small fire in the stone circle which, while it was part of the ceremony, seemed redundant in the summer heat. But he watched as the Wicasa Wikan, the Lakota tribal holy man, purified the air with the smoky sage, intoned a prayer as he turned to all four directions accompanied by the steady drumming of the musician. The Howe family had gifted the required tobacco and herbs to the holy man as well as to the two elders seated to the side, Takoda and Ray, who were silent and observing. The crowd, even the children, were still and respectful, and Jab was impressed by the attention the young ones gave. Additional prayers and drumming continued, and as Chaska held his small son, William, in his arms, the other three children stood quietly in front of their mother, Mina.

When the prayers and drumming, the offers of herbs and tobacco and fruit to the various spirits were done, the holy man nodded to Takoda and Ray, and the three of then stood together murmuring to each other in the Lakota language for some time. A soft wind blew through the trees under which the group stood, and Jab was grateful for it. Then the three elderly men stood facing the group. Takoda walked over to his son and held out his arms for William who went willingly to his grandfather. Walking to the center of the circle, Takoda turned the child to face the group and holding him outward, slowly turned around so all could get a look at the boy. Then he came back to Ray and the holy man and redeposited William into the arms of Chaska.

The holy man turned to the people and spoke one more prayer in the ancient language. He bowed his head, maintaining it momentarily, and when he looked up, he spoke in English.

"The tribal elders and I have determined the spirit name of the child who all have seen to be whole and healthy. Takoda tells me of his vision of the *hoka*, the badger, who is a healing medicine animal for young ones; an animal who is persistent and endures. Part of the boy's new name will be *Badger*. Ray dreams of his young son, Frank, the one who is already in the next world. His son was brave and courageous and through the dreams, spoke to Ray, saying that he imparted his great courage, his *chanjtesuta,* to the boy who struggled to be healthy. Part of the boy's new name will be *Brave*. As honor to Ray's dream of his son and in reverence to Takoda's vision, the name of the child will be: *William Frank Chanjtesuta Hoka Howe.* He is *Brave Badger.*"

The crowd erupted in yells and chants and claps, and Brave Badger hid his head on his father's shoulders until he saw his brother and sisters yelling and clapping. Then he joined in, and Mina held out her arms to the child she almost lost, and he went to his mother. The ceremony was ended.

A feast followed, and Jab sat on the ground with a plate overflowing with food brought to him by Mina who sat on the blanket feeding her children who were around her. Traditional foods, *wasna,* preserved meat, *blo,* wild potatoes, *wagmiza,* corn, was served along with hot dogs and hamburgers, and the women of the tribe provided platter after platter of foods. Chokecherry pudding and various berries filled another plate, and there was more than enough food on the long tables for the people who were there for the ceremony and the others who would attend later in the afternoon, after their jobs and chores and tasks were completed. Jab ate and watched the children and talked to Mina, and when he looked up, Chaska was waving to him to come over and join him and his cousin Tommy and a few other men Jab recognized.

The group greeted Jab as he came to where they were standing, and Chaska held out his hand and grabbed Jab's. He smiled at him and told the others about the stickball games he had given his children.

"A wonderful gift. All of them can share and play, and I will teach them how to play using the gift. Jab, you will need to come over and play with them. You show the spirit of *wacantognaka*, the generosity all Lakota believe in. Giving keeps the earth in balance, and we share. In the spirit of giving, please accept these," and Chaska handed some things to Jab.

Jab looked at the gifts from Chaska. There were two keychains. Both were intricately knotted with beads in the four direction colors: yellow, black, white, and red. The beads formed various shapes and symbols and the two keychains were individually and authentically decorated. Jab smiled at the gesture, admired both elaborately created items, and turned to Chaska to ask why he was given two.

Chaska put his hand on Jab's shoulder as he answered. "One is for you to use, and the other to keep until you know someone who is worthy. Then give it as a gift to that person to honor this day and my son, Brave Badger."

Jab thanked Chaska once more. A small wind blew, spreading the laughing of the children and the talking of the women, and the group of men led by Jab and Chaska, went into Tommy's large barn. Bottles were stored there in the large refrigerator. A cold one would taste good on such a warm summer day. The celebration would continue long into the night, long after the laughers and talkers were settled in sleep.

***

Jab held the reins loosely as he walked Tadita back to Tommy's barn where he would steadily and softly brush him. The horse was good tempered, calm, and gentle, and Jab appreciated that Tommy allowed him to visit the farm and ride the black and blanketed-white Appaloosa. This day's outing included a farewell ride. Jab would be leaving Pine Ridge in about a week. He had lived in the small apartment above Chaska's garage, had been part of the extended Howe family, had become friends with Chaska and Mina, Tommy and Donna, had spoken with and listened to Takoda for just over a year, had learned from his experiences in the town, and it was time to move on.

"You know," said Tommy as he offered Tadita water and watched Jab slowly brush the horse, "you are welcomed to stay here. I know the small garage apartment might not suit, and there is plenty of room in my house. My children are married with their own families and their rooms are available. I'm not that far from town, and you could ride Tadita whenever you weren't working. My wife likes you, and she suggested it to me. What do you think?"

Jab continued to rub and brush the horse. He lifted and checked the hooves before he spoke. He turned to Tommy and smiled at him. Jab had learned to take his time before speaking. One of the lessons from the past year.

"You are generous. Thanks to you and to Donna. I appreciate the offer, and if I were to stay longer, I might take you up on it. But I have stayed here longer than I planned, longer than I usually remain in a new place. Part of that was because I have enjoyed it so much. Chaska and Mina and the kids have become like family. You and Donna and the entire town have been generous and welcoming, and I will really miss my talks with Takoda. I learned much from him. But I need to go. It is time to move on," and Jab continued the brushing.

"Where will you go now?"

Jab stopped brushing but continued rubbing Tadita who nickered softly. "I'm never sure where I'll end up, but I'm going to head east. I haven't seen my own family, my mother and sister in a long time, and I think I'll visit for a while. My sister married some time ago, and I've never met her husband, so that is something I want to do. Also, I have an old friend I've recently been talking to. She's in Tennessee, and I think I want to visit her. I want to see her. Anyway, she's invited me, and eventually I'll get there," and Jab, who rarely spoke about his plans and had never mentioned his family, grew silent.

Tommy nodded. "When you finish here, come on up to the house. Donna always has something on the stove, and you should stay for one more meal before you go back to town."

"Thanks," and Jab continued to pat the horse. "I appreciate that. It will give me a chance to thank Donna and tell her good-bye. Be there in a few minutes."

Tommy turned to go and after a few steps, turned around again. "You know, in the Lakota language, there is no word for *good-bye*. The closest we come is *toksa akhe* and that translates to 'later, again'. I will see you later, again," and he left the barn.

Jab stood for a minute until Tadita shook his head as if to ask what was happening. He turned to the horse and rubbed between his eyes. He leaned his head against the horse's and considered the past months: the friendships, the enlightenment about the Lakota culture, the nurturing and growth, the wisdom gained from Takoda. Jab thought of his own moving restlessness and need to travel as he pressed into the animal he knew he would never ride again and whispered tenderly into his ear, "Toksa ache, Tadita. Toksa ache."

Takoda

He was present in my dreams for months, my oldest brother, Jak, who had left our parents' home many years ago and disappeared. I was the youngest, perhaps ten or twelve, when he left. No one ever saw him again. My mother would weep for him, and my father grew silent, and none of my sisters or brothers would talk about him to me. I wondered why he left and where he was and what happened to him, but it was only recently he appeared in my dreams. When Chaska brought the white man to our house, I recognized him. I knew that behind his eyes was my brother's spirit, my brother's restless being. Even his name was almost the same, and I called him by my oldest brother's name. He thought I was just pronouncing his white name incorrectly, but I knew who he was. He was my oldest brother, the one who appeared in my dreams, the man who came back in this life as a ghostly white man. He was Jak.

I said little to him at first. I only watched to see if it was Jak. I did not remember much from my childhood, and the only sister I have left is far away, living with her daughter, and she does not remember either. I asked her, but I did not tell her our brother had returned. She would be upset, and it was in my dreams and to me that Jak appeared. I did speak with Ray about my dreams and Jak's appearance, and we discussed why this man had come. Was he a good spirit? Was he one of the evil spirits, perhaps Gnas the trickster? I watched this man. I waited for another dream, but Jak was no longer in my dreams. He was here with me.

I went to Wicasa Wakun, gifting him the tobacco and herbs required. I told him of Jak and the disappearance. I spoke of my dreams of my brother. He said that Jak's *wanagi*, the spirit given to all at our creation, was not honored at his death and remained here. Purification was needed. I took his bundled sage and sweetgrass to Chakas's house, to all four corners, and gave the prayer for purification and protection. I gave the Four Directions Prayer, and then I waited. I waited and watched.

The white man, my brother, came and ate at our table. He was kind to Mina, my daughter, and to Chaska, her husband, and to the children. He was polite and brought foods to share and helped Chaska to replace the roof on the old house. He worked at the garage, repairing, and fixing. I waited and watched. I had no more dreams containing my eldest brother because my brother was here. His *wanagi* was strong and attached to this white man. I listened to him talk and watched when he was silent. He listened to Chaska and was considerate to Mina. He was gentle with the children. The purification and protection prayers were strong too, and I eased my mind and saw that this white man, my brother, wished to learn.

He would sit with me under the chokecherry tree in Chaska's yard, and because he was a white man, he had forgotten the stories. He listened, and I repeated the tales of the Lakota people. I told how all things had a spirit. All trees and rocks and animals. All people. I gave him the creation story. I told about the start of all, when Wakan Tanka was present and how Turtle helped bring clay to the Great Spirit who shaped the land and all the creatures. When White Buffalo Calf Woman brought the Sacred Pipe and gave instructions for its use and the ceremonies. How Small Bear was taught to fish and how Iktomi, teacher of wisdom, taught the people of good forces and of bad forces. And Jak listened and nodded and sometimes asked about the lessons which he had forgotten.

At times Ray and I would be together and Jak would sit and be with us. He was polite and knew that when we began to speak of private and sensitive things using Lakota language that it was time for him to go. He would leave, and Ray and I would talk about what was necessary and I would share my dreams. But now they did not contain my oldest brother. He was here. He was Jak. And I still waited and watched.

Under the chokecherry tree, I spoke to him of Lakota values, of *wacantognaka* and *wotitakuye*. Of *wacintaka* and *woksape*. Jak heard this, and I explained them; I told of the generosity and kinship. Of the bravery and wisdom which all Lakota children are taught. I told how all members of the tribe should care for each other, were taught to do this, and my sorrow that many did not live by the old ways but wanted the white man's culture and belief. I spoke of the sadness which had shown its face and stayed with so many in Pine Ridge, in the place we lived, in the land where we were poor and troubled by the evils the white man brought to us. I waited and watched to see if this white man, the brother who had forgotten his teachings, would turn angry and show an evil side; if he would become *wasicu witko*. He did not. Jak listened and I could tell that he was not the crazy white man. He was Jak. My oldest brother.

I relaxed and began to enjoy the teaching of him. He would bring me small gifts. Knowing my fondness for the maple candy from the town, he would bring it to me. I liked the ice cream from town, and Jak would bring it for the grandchildren and me, and we would sit under the tree at night and I would talk, and he would listen, and we would eat the melting treat he had brought. There were times nothing was said, and we would be still and enjoy the quiet of the approaching dark. We would sit and watch as Thate, the wind spirit, moved the leaves of the chokecherry tree. We would watch the night come, and when it was time, he would go, and I would sleep, and no dreams would come.

He asked about my markings, my tattoos. I would show and explain to him their importance. I told him how the Sky-Road which is where the dead go, was guarded by *Hihankaga*. The dead must show the proper marks, or they may not enter into the next life but are sent to wander the earth as ghosts. And when I said this, when I showed my marks, when I told Jak that they were sacred and specific to me, I realized why he had returned to me. I asked him if there were markings he had, but he said there were none. When he said this, then I understood. This is the reason. This is what happened. My eldest brother, Jak, had died without receiving the proper marks. His wanagi was not honored. He was not allowed into the Sky-Road, the next life. He was returned to the earth to wander. This was the reason for his ghost. I understood. I had waited and watched, and I understood.

It was not for me to encourage him to receive the marks, but now I knew the answer. I will try to make it right. I will help my ghost brother to go to the next life. I will get one more mark on my body and when my time to enter the Sky-Road comes, I will show it to Hihankaga, the owl-maker, and tell her I have my eldest brother's mark on me, that he should now be allowed to enter, that I have undertaken the task for him, and he is now purified. His wandering will be done.

I cannot do it until Jak leaves. I know he will not stay because his spirit is a restless one. He must travel. That is his fate. When he told Chaska and then he came to me to say he would be leaving, I was both sad and at ease. Once he is gone, I will have Chaska take me to the place where I will have one more mark on my lower right leg. It will be the *Kapemni* which is the Lakota symbol and looks like two triangles resting on each other. The top triangle stands for the sun and the stars; the bottom one for the earth. There is a connection between the two, just as there is a connection between my eldest brother and me and a connection between his time as an earth ghost and his place in the Sky-Road. When my time comes to go to the next life, I will show Hihankaga that my brother's mark is on me. I will wait for him and watch for his return to the Sky-Road. We will be together and the spirits of our parents and our brothers and sisters will be eased. This is why I dreamed of Jak. This is why the white man came to Pine Ridge. This is why the white man wanders. He is the restless ghost of Jak. Chaska will understand and will take me for the last mark I must have. I will say the prayer of purification and protection for the ghost of Jak. I will hope he finds some peace in this earth life, that he will receive some stillness into his soul. And I will wait. And I will watch.

7. Woman's Scarf
Meri

Oh, love isn't there to make us happy.
I believe it exists to show us how much we can endure.

From Hesse's *Peter Camenzind*

It was at least ten years since Jab and I had seen each other. He stayed in touch, usually by telephone, although he was in the habit of sending postcards or brief notes periodically. I received a dozen or so through the years, but I'm unsure how many I missed, how many were lost in the mail, or were thrown out by old addresses, from places I no longer lived. The phone calls were brief, only about five minutes, and nothing of importance was said, except he thought about me and hoped we would meet again. I never told him I had been married. That wasn't a discussion we had time for in the five minutes we spoke. And then I didn't hear from him for a long time. When he called Jen and asked about me, she told him that after my divorce, I had moved to Tennessee to stay with a cousin who lived there. Jen told me he said "Divorce?" in a shocked tone, and she only then realized he hadn't been told about my marriage. I told her that was fine and not to worry about it, and that I'd probably never hear from him again, even though he asked for, and she gave him, my new phone number and address. But I did.

Jab called when he was in South Dakota. Twice. He called when he was in Iowa, and then in Missouri. He called right before he saw his family and then, after he left the Chicago area and was traveling to Mark's place, he called. He called from Waterville where he was staying. That was the longest phone call, the most intense.

"So Mark is gone?"

"Yep. A woman he knew came back to the farm and they decided to travel together. He sold the place, and they left a while ago for California. Someone said they got married, but I don't know for sure. His place looks different, and there is a large family with four or five kids living there. Waterville has changed. It's expanded, and there were few people I knew from the past. The Watering Hole is still there, but Hank sold it and there are different owners. They didn't need a bartender or any other help."

"You asked?"

"I did. I thought I might stay around for a time, but it looks like I'll be coming your way sooner than I thought. Still interested in seeing me?"

I laughed. "Yes, Jab, still interested. But I'm moving out of my cousin's place in a couple weeks. Got a new job about an hour north of Nashville in Cleary. I've rented a place, but it won't be ready for a couple weeks, so right now I'm commuting for my job. I can give you the address, but no phone number yet. I'll leave the info with Barb, and when you can call in a few weeks, I should be moved in."

"That will work. Let's say three weeks. Will you be settled by then?"

"Should be."

"Great. Tell Barb I'll call her."

We spoke for a few minutes longer and then hung up. Honestly, I wondered if I would ever hear from or see him again, but I told Barb to expect a call. And then I added that possibly there would be none. I moved out a couple weeks later, got settled in Cleary, Tennessee, organized my life, and I wasn't surprised when over a month later, I still hadn't heard from Jab.

It was almost two months later, on a late Monday night, that he called. I had made a quick dinner and was finishing up the dishes and considering going to bed earlier than usual despite some moving boxes which still needed to be emptied. The phone rang. It was Jab. I was both glad and aggravated.

"I know," he explained, "that I said I'd call about a month ago, but I got caught up with some old friends. Remember Buzz? I met up with him and stayed with him and his family for a time. He's married with a couple kids, and still plays the drums but isn't traveling full time with the band. He still keeps in touch with the other guys and now and then meets them for a quick gig. They are going to be in Nashville in another month, and Buzz said he knows a bunch of people there. He arranged for me to work at a couple of the small venues along Lower Broadway. They are temporary jobs, but I'm here now, staying in Nashville. At least for a while."

"Why didn't you call when you got in to town?"

"Just got in Friday, and they needed me to work right away. It's been a busy weekend, and today was the first day I had some time to find a place to stay. The one venue let me crash in the backroom where there was a bed, but I couldn't stay there long. Anyway, I have a couple days off and would like to see you. Is that possible?"

We made plans to meet the following evening, and I gave Jab directions to my Cleary apartment. I told him I'd just order something for dinner, and we'd catch up. "Still have the bike?" I asked.

"Not right now. I've had a truck for a while, but thinking about trading it in for a bike. Maybe in a few months. Where can I park when I get there?"

We talked for a few minutes more and then hung up. I looked around. There were still too many boxes which needed to be unpacked, so I decided to forget about getting to bed early and went about finishing my moving in. While I put things away and broke down the boxes, I thought about Jab and wondered how and if he had changed.

I had no trouble recognizing him the next day although he looked different. He was older, but then we both were. His beard was gone and his hair was cut short and it was graying on the sides. I kept staring at him because I had never seen him without a beard. I asked why he had shaved it.

"I'm just a …*wave to fit whatever form I take…*" he quoted and smiled.

We had a great time, and within minutes, it was as though we hadn't been apart for all those years. I told him he could stay overnight on the couch if he wanted to, but he said he needed to get back. There were some things he needed to get done the next day, so about midnight, we said good-night, and he left. I watched out of my front window as he walked to his truck, and when he turned back, we waved to each other. Perhaps that should have been the extent of our relationship, but it wasn't. It was only the beginning.

For close to two months Jab and I rarely saw each other. He was busy in Nashville and continued working the weekends. Then Buzz came to town to be with his old band friends, and Jab spent time with them. He and I would meet for a quick dinner now and then because my job was keeping me busy too. I was getting used to living in Cleary and had made some new friends and was getting to know them. Once I drove into Nashville to visit one of the music venues where Jab and Buzz were, but they were busy, and I didn't stay long. I wasn't sure if Jab would be staying in the area for any length of time. I knew it was his habit to move around. So, I was surprised when he called and said he was moving to Cleary because his jobs at the venues were over, and he was moving out of Nashville. He had gotten a position working at the large home improvement center just outside of town. He was going to look for small place to stay or see if someone at work would rent him a room or needed a roommate, but for the time, was the offer of my couch still open? I said it was, and he moved in temporarily. Well, that was the plan.

I'm not blaming Jab for anything that happened. I take responsibility. He made it clear and was absolutely sincere in his decision to stay just until he found another place. He had a regular schedule and was often gone before I even woke up in the mornings, and on those early days he would be home before me and would have made dinner for us. After a week or so, as we sat at the table eating, he told me that he was pretty sure he would be moving out in a few days.

"This guy at work, Justin, said his roommate was going to move out of the apartment and in with his girlfriend. He said I could take over his spot and move in. There's one other roommate, and I haven't met him yet, but Justin said he travels with his job, so part of the time he isn't even there. I'll be out of your hair in less than a week, I hope. I really appreciate you letting me stay here, Meri."

I took a last bite of the dinner and chewed slowly, giving myself added time to think. Jab was easy to live with. He was quiet and thoughtful, and not even messy. He traveled light and had few belongings, so there wasn't much clutter around. And the apartment was large for a one-bedroom. There was a roomy walk-in closet off the bathroom and I hadn't filled it up. I thought about what I was going to say and hesitated, but said it anyway.

"Listen, Jab. If you want, you can stay here. We can get a mattress for the walk-in closet, and you can sleep in there if you want to. I like your company, and we get along, and I won't mind sharing. We've been OK for the past few days, and I'll be fine with whatever you want to do. It's up to you, but I just want to make the offer."

Jab looked at me and sat still for a time. "Are you sure?" he asked.

"I am," and we discussed the logistics of his moving in, the finances we would share, and by the end of the evening, it had been decided. Jab moved in.

***

We got along. We liked many of the same things; reading, music, discussions. Jab found an old guitar at a second-hand store, bought it, restrung it, and began to play again. Our schedules gave us alone time at the apartment, so we weren't always bumping into each other. I would go out with my friends, and Jab would sometimes travel to Nashville for the music. At times, we would go together and walk the streets going from one bar to another, listening to music and eating the various foods offered at stands along the way. We lived together as friends, as a platonic couple, as roommates. There was no discussion or attempt at a romantic relationship. Until there was.

It was a Sunday night, and I was reading on the couch as Jab sat in the corner of the room plunking on the guitar. We had spent Saturday night in Nashville listening to music for hours, walking along the streets and talking. The night went on, and in the early morning we returned, stopping for pancakes at an all-night diner a few streets from the apartment. We ate and talked, and when we walked into the apartment, the sun was just rising, and we were exhausted. I went to my bedroom and lay down, and Jab went into the closet which had become his bedroom. We slept for hours, and when I got up, it was late afternoon and Jab was gone. I took a shower and redressed and when I went into the kitchen to make coffee, Jab was there putting away groceries and asking if I was hungry. We worked together making a meal and talking about the music from the previous night. We shared the cleaning up, after which I settled down to read, and Jab began to play quietly on the guitar. In a while, he began to talk.

"You've never talked about being married, Meri. And I suppose it's none of my business, but why didn't you ever say anything to me? Were you married long?"

I marked the place in my book and looked at him. "No, I wasn't. It was a mistake for both of us. We worked together at Hopper's and became friendly and then started to date. We dated for months, and then one night, the idea of marriage came up, and we just decided to do that. It was a very small wedding, just his sister and her family and a few of our mutual friends, and we found a small apartment together. But we were so different and didn't realize it until we lived together. I liked to read, and he didn't understand how I could sit so long with a book. He wanted to go to every new movie that came out, and I was fine just seeing a few a year. I liked eggs, and he said they made him sick. He would only listen to country music, and while I don't mind it, I wanted to hear a variety of music. The differences were small, but they added up, and by the end of a year, we knew that marriage was a mistake, so we divorced. Nothing dramatic. We parted in a friendly manner, and he left to go somewhere out west, I think to Washington State. I didn't want to stay in the apartment, so when the lease was up, I sold most of the things and came out here to stay with Barb. A failed experiment," and I shrugged.

Jab listened and nodded. "OK. Thanks for telling me. Don't mean to pry, but I was curious. Never been close to marriage myself. Think it would be a mistake given my natural inclination to travel like I do."

"You haven't told me about all your travels. Where else have you been? What have you done?"

Jab grinned and began to talk. He spoke for almost two hours, explaining the last dozen or so years. He told me of his various jobs: bartender, cook, dish-washer, delivery truck driver, farm-hand, mechanic. He admitted there were fights or arguments he got in, and periodically would need to leave a place in the middle of the night. There were some card games during which he won a lot of money, and other games he lost everything. He talked about the people he had known and how he had learned from them, and how Mangas and Takoda influenced him and taught him about their culture and beliefs. He spoke of women he knew and one or two he stayed with for a while. He told me of the horses he had learned to ride and the beauty of the outside world and his sadness that his mother had died but he did not know it, and his happiness at meeting the good man his sister had married, and his joy at a nephew whose middle name was his. I learned more about him in those two hours than I ever had and realized I was still attracted to him. When he was silent, I took a chance and reminded him of the things he had said to me once, of the sweetness spoken. When he listened and replied that his feelings had not changed, but he had no intentions of pursuing an unwanted relationship, I knew that he would no longer sleep in the walk-in closet that had been his bedroom.

***

We became a couple. We slept in the same bed, cleaned the small apartment together, went to the grocery store and music venues together, talked about the highs and lows of our jobs as we made dinner together, and my friends accepted us as a twosome. The months passed, and we welcomed our intimacy and were content. We spent Saturday nights in Nashville, listening to music and seeing friends we had made, walking down the streets, and visiting shops. One time, I stopped to admire some of the scarves and jewelry in the window of a boutique, and a couple days later, when I came him from work, the scarf I noticed and remarked about was laying across the bed. It was maroon and gold, and lilies which are my favorite flower, were spread across the edge and bits of green leaves were sprinkled throughout. I smiled and picked it up to tie in my hair, the ends of it drifting down one shoulder. Jab smiled when he saw it, and I wore it every Saturday we visited Nashville, sometimes like a headband and sometimes wrapped around my pony tail. When Jab did leave, I tied the scarf around his neck, a totem, a trinket to keep him safe.

He had been with me close to a year, and I could see a restlessness in him that worried me. He would rise early in the morning, and I would find him staring out the window, looking into the distance. At times, he would say he wanted to go for a walk and would be back in an hour, but two or three would pass, and he returned, apologizing for not paying attention to the time. He would begin to play the guitar, and then stop and stare down at it, lost in thought, and not answering when I spoke to him. I felt there was going to be an end to this co-habitation of ours, and I didn't want it to end, but I also didn't want him to be unhappy, and that seemed to be his prevailing mood.

One day he came home from a long ride he had taken. He clutched a small brown bag in his hands. He reached in and pulled the small pink moccasins he had bought at some tourist place and explained why he had them.

"I called my sister, and she is going to have another baby. I told her it was going to be a girl, and she just laughed and asked how I could possibly know. I'm going to send these to her. Is there a small box around?"

I searched and came up with an appropriately sized one, and watched while he drilled a small hole in the bottom of one shoe and got the package ready to send.

"OK. What's the reason for that? And how do you know this baby is going to be a girl? Do you have special powers I don't know about?"

He laughed and told me of a Native American tradition. A small hole was created in one of the moccasins so that evil spirits would be fooled. This would protect the small child because she could not travel far with a hole in the bottom of the moccasin. She could not go to the land of the dead. He was protecting his soon-to-be niece. He looked at me and tilted his head and grinned.

"Sometimes I just know things," he laughed, and I stored this comment away in my mind.

It was a month or so after that he grew extremely quiet. I knew something was going to change and waited for him to tell me. When we spoke one evening after eating dinner and doing the dishes together, he said he was going to leave for a time. He didn't say he would return, but he didn't say he wouldn't. I wasn't surprised, only saddened. I expected this, but it didn't make his leaving easier.

"Where are you headed?"

Jab shrugged. "I'm not sure. I know that there are things I want to see and do, and I know I'm getting older, and need to do them now. Maybe out west again. Maybe up towards Kentucky or east. I might visit my sister again," and he sighed before looking at me and taking my hand. "I wish I could stay, and maybe one day I will, but not now. I know this is upsetting, and I'm sorry. There has been no one else except you, and if I ever settle down, it will be with you. Can you understand?"

I did. And I didn't. I said I understood. At least I tried to.

"When will you go?"

"Soon," he answered. "This week. Maybe in a day or two. I just want to check out the truck and get a few things together," and he hugged me. I didn't mean to, but I cried.

Two days later, on a Sunday morning, he was up, gathering a few things and finishing packing his duffel bag. Jab had always traveled light, and there was little to pack. He went to the truck to place some things in it, and then came back to the apartment. We stood holding each other for a while, and I tied the lily scarf around his neck.

"There. Now you will be safe and won't forget me," and I held back tears. I meant to be strong although, afterwards, I would spend much of that Sunday sobbing into my bed, keeping a secret to myself. I knew if I told it, I could keep him with me, but I had decided that he should only stay if it was his decision.

"Never," he murmured into my neck, "I'll never forget you. And I'll be back. I promise to stay in touch. I promise," and then he whispered the words I wanted him to whisper, and I said them back, and we stayed like that, two of us pressed into one.

There was no more discussion. One more kiss. He left. I peeked out the window and watched him get into the truck. He hesitated before he got in but didn't turn around. Instead, he lifted his hand in my direction, knowing I would be watching. Then he got into the truck, started it, and pulled out, driving slowly down the empty street while a lone early morning church bell sounded, signaling farewell. I watched until it was impossible to see any part of him or his truck, and when the street was bare once again, I went to the couch and sat down. Morning was just developing, and I thought about going back to bed, but I couldn't do that just yet. I didn't want to enter the bedroom where we had spent one last night together. I didn't want to put my face on the sheets and smell his scent. Not yet. I had to think.

I thought back to his prediction about his sister's baby, to his definitive assurance that he knew it would be a girl, that he sometimes *just knows things,* to his almost smug attitude, and then said out loud to the air, "No, Jab, you don't *just know things*. Not always," and I gathered my hands just below my belly button where I was protecting a secret.

8. Pack of Playing Cards

You had to learn to see man as a weak, selfish, and cowardly creature; you also had to realize how many of these evil traits and impulses you shared yourself...

W*isteria Sinensis*, commonly known as *Chinese Wisteria,* is a hardy, graceful, aggressive, long-lived plant whose flowers have a vibrant sometimes overpowering scent which, according to folklore, can work as a demon repellent, and when their season is over, drop, causing a slimy mess. All parts of the plant are toxic. Children in the eponymously named Wisteria, West Virginia, are cautioned against picking it up from their gardens, and numerous pet dogs die yearly from grabbing and chewing on the plant's pods. It can be considered invasive, needing yearly pruning and careful control, although there is no denying the beauty of the arbors which are decorated with the crawling vines, or the intense perfume of the hanging branches of the gnarled trunks which line the main street of the town. No one recollects which early town settlers created the woody tree-lined walkways, and past attempts by various civic minded gardening architects to rid the town of the toxic trees proved unsuccessful. Roots reached deep into the underground, refusing to die, resurrecting in legendarily Biblical fashion, so the paths to the main streets remained mellow and malevolent, picturesque and perilous, lovely and lethal. Wisteria, West Virginia. The town in which Jab had settled.

It had taken a while for Jab to get there after leaving Tennessee because he didn't travel in a straight line. He revisited his past: in Texas, then back to Missouri, then into Illinois, stopping to abide and work, when necessary, occasionally gambling, often winning, sometimes losing. He tinkered with whatever vehicle he was driving to keep it running, picked up thrift store clothes and books, discussed ideas with roadside-bar companions. He considered what to do and where to go next; he wrote postcards and sent gifts to his sister and her family. He missed Meri. He thought about her, sending her the occasional brief letter or postcard. There were dozens of times, ready with pocketed change, he entered a pay phone booth, picked up the black receiver, and began to dial her phone number, always hanging up before he dialed more than three or four digits although once he let it ring twice before hanging up.

He called himself *selfish* and *weak*. He labeled himself a *coward*, and he lived with those thoughts and appellations until the next time he got up some nerve to enter a telephone booth, pockets filled with quarters. And failed again to dial the fifth digit of the number.

Eventually Jab traveled back through Tennessee, thinking that he was ready to see Meri. His courage was back, his strength determined, his spirit magnanimous. He parked in front of Meri's apartment and after wiping sweaty palms on jeans for the fifth or sixth time, after walking slowly to her apartment, after waiting patiently for the answer to his decisive knock, the door was opened and he was informed by a strange man that the woman he had come to face was gone. Moved on to somewhere else, somewhere unknown, taking her sofa and her dresser and her secret with her in a rented truck, pulling her car behind her. Perhaps to Ohio or Indiana. Not sure. Jab thanked him and then sat in his car for an hour before deciding to search out one of Meri's friends who refused to greet him in a pleasant manner, was annoyed at his questions, and remained markedly unfriendly as she stood in her doorway only telling him that, yes, she went back home to Indiana, and he had some nerve coming here, and then shutting the door and locking it with a loud *Damn it!* Jab stood for a while, uncertain as to what he did to cause such rancor, and then, returning to his truck, aimed it towards Kentucky, traveled through, refusing the temptation to stop, and finally landing in Wisteria, West Virginia, home of the hardy and toxic. It suited his mood, and he did what he had always done: set down tentative roots which were nothing like those of the Wisteria plants whose refusal to expire remained spectral.

Jab rented a room in a large Victorian house where the upper floor housed two other men who were, like Jab, just traveling through. The older man, Gil, had been just traveling through for a dozen years now, telling Jab that the town, Wisteria, was a good place *not* to settle down and explaining, at length, the reasons why. The younger man, Andy, was not as friendly, although he was more than willing to share a bottle of Four Roses Kentucky Bourbon with his flat mates on the Fridays he got paid. Of course, he expected Gil and Jab to support his habit on the alternate Fridays when he didn't get paid, and it became a tradition: sharing a bottle, playing cards, and discussing consequential ideas in the backyard of the old Victorian house when weather permitted. They would set up the rusty card table and semi-erect chairs behind the collapsing shed and against the wooden fence where the wisteria vines grew up and around the pickets, keeping them stationary and alert while partially hiding the men from the view of Mrs. Grannet, the proprietor of the Victorian boarding house. Not that she would have minded, but Gil was fairly certain that the woman, a hefty widow about ten years older than Gil, who kept her own bottle of Four Roses in her butler's pantry, was after him, ready, willing, and anxious to remarry at the slightest suggestion. Gil shivered at the thought.

"Mrs. Grannet has been after me since I moved in," he explained every Friday evening, "and I heard she poisoned her old man for his fortune." He sucked in the tubular Marlboro, allowing the smoke to enter deeply into his lungs, helping foster the burgeoning cancer cells which would complete their work within the following years, expelling what was left and coughing until his breath, his wheezing breath, could be heard once again. He only smoked on Fridays, he had explained, although Jab could see his head hanging out from the upstairs window nightly, completing the exercise numerous times. Neither Jab nor Andy complained. There were few enough pleasures.

They were entertaining companions, willing to listen to Jab expound upon various philosophical and metaphysical concepts, then eagerly questioning him about the ideas. They played cards, sometimes betting small amounts, and asked questions and made comments between sips of Four Roses, and Jab enjoyed his time in the wisteria choked yard where the scented foliage almost masked the aroma of Gil's Marlboros.

"So, this guy says that a person can DREAM stuff and still be awake?" and Andy, skeptic he was, took another swallow of his drink, and called for two more cards. He placed his rejected cards face down, picked up the ones Gil shifted to him, looked at them and said, "I'm out." He poured himself two more fingers of the Four Roses.

"Ha!" and Gil, "What do you have Jab? That Carlos guy is nuts. Can't be awake and asleep at the same time. Man! You win again!" and he threw down the cards and lit up another cigarette.

Jab pulled the pile of pennies and nickels towards him and explained, "It's called *lucid dreaming*, and it's not done while you are awake. It just means you know you're dreaming while you are asleep,"

Gil coughed smoke from his mouth, pointed to the bottle which Andy passed to him and poured himself the last of the liquid which he hoped would soothe his throat. Then he sat back and shook his head. "Don't know, Jab. How do you come up with all these ideas? Some sound downright strange. Gotta be all that reading you do. Never read much myself; that was a problem with me and school, but I guess some do like to read. Hey, Andy, any more peanuts left?"

Andy picked up the bag which was empty. He held it out for the other two men to see, and then said, "How about walking to Jilly's for some pepperoni rolls? Gil? Jab? Not too late, and I could go for something besides peanuts."

"Sounds good to me. Jab? How about it?"

Jab shrugged his shoulders, "Sure, why not? Let's put this table away and take a walk. Nice night to do it."

Gill stood up and stretched and folded his chair. They moved the card table and the chairs against the shed, picked up the empty peanut bag and whiskey bottle which Andy threw into the garbage can just outside the rickety picket fence, and Jab stacked their empty, chipped tea cups under the chairs. They walked out of the back gate and down the street towards the main town, towards Jilly's which was known for the hot and crusty pepperoni rolls which, served with chilled Mountain Dew, was the embodiment of a West Virginian feast.

As they walked, Gil said, "You won big tonight, Jab. You buy."

Jab shrugged his shoulders and grinned. "Sure, Gil. I'll buy," and as they turned left onto Main Street, the wisteria vines fluttered and swayed in the early night breeze, dispatching the essence of a vindictive pungency.

***

Jab did not work Friday nights or Sunday nights, but his three part-time jobs kept him busy the remainder of the time. Most days he worked for Harold at Harold's Repair Shop where he rebuilt, restored, and reconditioned everything from lawn mowers to coffee pots to electronic gadgets. Then many nights he worked as a fry cook at the diner just out of town, at the eastern end of Wisteria's Main Street. Late Saturday and Monday nights, and sometimes, after working the diner on Wednesday and Thursday nights, and depending upon shipments received, he restocked the shelves at the local Piggly Wiggly. He earned money to support himself, to pay his rent, to buy the occasional bottle of Four Roses, to purchase foodstuffs, to acquire used books at the local thrift stores, and to lightly gamble with Gil and Andy. He saved the remainder of his earnings. First, he had a debt to pay back, and second, well, he wasn't sure why, but he knew there was a reason to save. There was an inkling of a nudging of a reason. He was aware that sometimes he just knew things although what he knew wasn't clear. Jab worked and spent Friday nights with the two men who had become his friends,

Sunday mornings hiking alone into the nearby mountains or sight-seeing in his truck, and sometimes, just sometimes on Sunday nights, he took Brenda, the older divorced woman who clerked at the Piggly Wiggly to a music concert, a dinner, and occasionally, the next morning, to breakfast.

Wisteria, West Virginia is found along the Ohio River, in the foothills of the Appalachian Mountains. It's about seventy miles west of Pittsburg, Pennsylvania, and if one travels west on Interstate 70, about one hundred thirty miles, Columbus, Ohio appears. Jab knew this from his several early Sunday morning trips to both places. Pittsburg was closer, but Columbus interested him more. He was content staying in Wisteria for a time, but knew it would not be forever. *I just can't seem to stay in one place*, he often chided himself.

The months passed. Summer, then fall and winter, and now it was spring again. The weather was temperate and tranquil for a Sunday morning, and Jab woke up with an itch to get out in it. He completed his morning ablutions, readied himself for a hike, and quietly left the old Victorian house where various sibilate snuffles could be heard coming from both upstairs and downstairs. Mrs. Grannet was not excused. He went to the kitchen, filled up his plastic water bottle from the sink, carefully closed the door behind him, and got into his truck which transported him to his favorite mountainous spot.

He parked, locked the truck, and began his trudge up the side of the slope which was just beginning to be covered with the lime-green colored spring grasses between the rocks; thus, the path was not too slippery. He had been here before. He knew where he would go and which rock he would rest upon, and what he would see as he looked out at the vista before him. Jab arrived to the flattened rock and sat down. He took a swig of the water from the bottle, and sighed deeply with contentment, with the pleasure of his solitude and the ease in his core. These times in nature were succor and solace to him, an abatement of his weekly thoughts and worries, a consolation from his self-condemnation for real and imagined sins. Jab used these times to consider and contemplate, to remember and reflect. He sat and watched as the sun grew and the heat of early spring collected around his head causing small beads of sweat to appear just at the edges of his scalp. He remembered his parents and his sister. He smiled at the vision of his nephew and his niece. He grew delighted at the recollection of Meri, and then sober at the recollection of Meri. He should call her, but he didn't know her phone number or exactly where she was in Indiana. He should call some of her friends and find out. He rebuked himself for the coward he was, for his weakness and his selfishness. A deep exhalation left his lungs, and he glanced up at the day. He rose, finished the water in his bottle, and walked back to the truck. It was time to return.

***

Jab stayed in Wisteria for almost two years. He was shocked when he realized how long he had been in one spot, and thought that perhaps he might even stay longer. But he didn't. Things had changed in the old Victorian house. Andy had left. He said that his sister had contacted him, wanting to see him, and offering him a home. He needed to go. Jab and Gil held a farewell dinner for him a couple days before he left for good. The three of them put on clean shirts, combed their hair, cleaned under their nails, and once arrayed in their finery, piled into Jab's truck. In about thirty minutes, they arrived at the Mountain View Resort and Casino where they planned to do a small snippet of gambling, a moderate modicum of eating, and a hearty hunk of drinking. They succeeded at all, and Jab spent some of his saved cash to rent a room at the nearby hotel for the night. Driving home to Mrs. Grannet's domicile was not an option.

The following morning, ingesting a meal of softly scrambled eggs, greasy potatoes, and both bacon and sausage whose additional grease was sopped up with soft biscuits, made them all feel like living again. Jab lifted his third cup of hot coffee and toasted his companions.

"To you, Andy; to a safe trip and happy time with your family. And to friendship," and the three of them clicked their coffee cups which was reminiscent of the clicking of their shot glasses the previous evening although with fewer consequences.

"Thank you, Jab. Thank you, Gil. This has been a great farewell. I'll miss you both, and who knows, perhaps I'll be back this way. I hope so, but who knows what the future will bring?"

Andy grew additionally sober at the realization that he may never see the other two men again. And he never would. Within a short time, Jab would move on. Gil would remain at Mrs. Grannet's abode where, in the coming year, she would move him downstairs to the empty bedroom next to hers and nurse him through the illness which would ravage his body. Gil would realize he owed her and would feel a gratefulness to her. Before leaving for the afterlife, he would make Mrs. Grannet blush with girlish pleasure by lying to her. "If I only had more time," he would say, "we could be married." He had been reassured by the doctor that such an inconveniency would not happen, so he was generous in his deceit.

Another man took Andy's place, but he was not sociable, and the drinking and card playing never resumed. When Jab packed his duffel bag to go, he picked up the pack of playing cards and, walking to Gil's room, quietly knocked on the door. When Gil appeared, enveloped in a cloud of tobacco smoke, Jab held the pack out to him.

"Here, Gil. Maybe you'll find another group to play cards. You should keep these."

Gil shook his head. He coughed a mighty cough and answered, "No, Jab. Don't think so. My card playing days are done. Keep them for the next set of friends. Besides, you always won! That's your lucky deck."

Jab smiled and they spoke for a while, repeated their good-byes, and shook hands several times. When he returned to his room to check once more that nothing was left behind, Jab unzipped his packed bag and placed the pack of cards at the bottom. He would never play with them again, but would keep them as a commemorative.

Jab walked down the stairs to Mrs. Grannet's parlor where she was busy interviewing his replacement. He waved to her since he had already said his formal good-byes. She waved back. He went out to his truck, opened the passenger side, placed his duffel bag and a paper bag on the seat, then walked around to the driver's side. Before he got in, he glanced up at the old Victorian house. There, at an upper window, Gil's head could be seen, a Marlboro dangling from his mouth. Gil removed it, expelled the whiteness, coughed a shuddery cough, and saluted Jab with the hand that cradled the cigarette. Jab saluted back, nodded, and got into the truck. As he dove away from Wisteria, West Virginia, he rolled down his window, and one last time, breathed in the air which was crowded with the redolent essence of *Wisteria Sinensis*.

Gil

Gilbert Edward Winslow. Quite a handle for a scrungy old man, but sometimes I need to remind myself who I am. Or maybe who I was. Past tense. My name is a family gift, a proud heritage I never lived up to. Apparently, a Gilbert Winslow came over on the Mayflower. He didn't stay, but went back to England to live a solitary life and die there; however, his brother, Edward, and another one or two brothers or cousins remained in the New World, settling down, creating the family from which I am descended. A proud heritage indeed, but I didn't deserve it, didn't warrant it. My father told me that every time he lectured me after another "incident". I agreed with him, and after my third failed attempt at obtaining a sheepskin from college, I was banished from the family compound in upper New York state where my family has resided in isolated splendor for generations. I willingly left and made my way to the closest army recruitment office and joined up, willing to fight in the war that was ending. I spent my two years in misery at Camp Drum in the northern regions of New York where I helped to guard the few prisoners of war who were there. After I was honorably discharged, I left, stopping at my family's large house only to engage in one last profound argument with my father, and then I departed for good.

I traveled and lived all over, working a job here and there, silently grateful to the yearly check my mother secretively arranged to send me which kept me from total destitution many times. I once or twice had an old automobile which assisted my travels and adventures, but most of the time, I tramped around, wearing out the cheap shoes I continually bought. I spent years traveling through New York, Pennsylvania, and Virginia. I wandered through the Carolinas, Tennessee, and Kentucky, and while there, married a pretty waitress and lived for a time in a small town just outside of Bowling Green. As much as I had traveled in the South, it was a shock to realize that the Confederacy was still going strong there. Tough for a born Northerner. But when my wife realized I was not the gung-ho worker who would be willing to support her and a large family, she divorced me. I worked my way to this place, West Virginia, and liked it. That's one reason Jab and I got along. Essentially, we are kindred spirits, although I think he is more of a migrator that I ever was. And now, I've been here, in Wisteria for about a dozen years, living on the small check I continue to receive due to my mother's iron-clad *Last Will and Testament* and the earnings from whatever periodic jobs a sixty-five-year-old man can find. It's enough.

Keeps me in the pepperoni rolls, the bi-weekly bottle of Four Roses and the Marlboros I became addicted to in the army. And pays the small amount of rent due on the fifteenth of each month to Mrs. Grannet which allows me to live in one of the three rooms she rents out to men like me and Jab and Andy who prefer to live on the fly. Well, not so much me. Think I very well could be stuck here the remainder of my life. Not such a bad thing.

I recognized Jab's essence as soon as we were introduced. I asked a few questions and noted the restraint and selectiveness of his answers and knew him. Knew he was a wanderer like me, and he would be secretive about his life and his experiences. I didn't push him, but during the time we got to know each other, he came to trust me. Who was I going to tell his secrets to? Who would he tell mine to? We trusted each other, and one Friday night, after we had played cards and shared the bottle of whiskey, Andy strode off to bed saying he had work in the morning, although if he did, he never got there having finished off most the bottle himself. Jab and I stayed in the yard and talked. It was a typically pleasant night in Wisteria, and we sat back, having nowhere to go, and no money to spend, and drank the glasses of sweet tea Jab brought out for us from the kitchen where Mrs. Grannet kept a jug. We talked about the card game which Andy had finally won, mentioning he had, once again, cheated, and while we both knew it, neither of us had cared enough to call him on it. We mentioned the fact that the three churches in town were planning a "Wisteria's All Churches Social and Picnic" on Sunday and wondered if the food to be shared was worth the price of admission: listening to three sermons. We decided it was too expensive for our tastes. We sat in the old folding chairs, content, sipping the tea, and watching the darkness come. I felt a need to confide in Jab, so I told him something I hadn't told anyone else, not even Andy.

"Y'all know," I began in the twangy way I had adopted, "I was married once." I waited for his shocked look and disbelieving "What!?"

Jab took a sip of his tea and waited for a few seconds before be answered. "OK."

I glanced at him, but he wasn't baiting me. He simply accepted what I told him and waited to hear more. Or not. I continued.

"She was a waitress in Martinsville, a small place right south of Bowling Green. I stayed there for a while. Had a job for a time at one of the large farms and would go into the town to eat now and then at the diner. Her name was Milly and she had reddish hair and a cute upturned nose, and we got along."

Jab nodded. "Obviously it didn't last."

I snickered. "No, Sir. We married after a few months and rented a small place. I tried to settle down and be the husband she wanted, but we weren't suited to each other after all. Lasted almost two years, and most of the last year she was gone back living with her parents and back working in the restaurant where we met. One day, her older brother showed up at the farm where I was working, handed me some papers, and told he to sign. I didn't argue. No sense in that. So, I signed them, handed them back, and he hauled off and *tried to beat some sense into me*…at least that's what he said. I wasn't ready for it, and took a beating so bad that some of the other farmhands wanted me to call the sheriff. But I figured that was my due, so I let it go, quit the farm, and left the area. Eventually ended up here. Learned my lesson. No more marriage for me, so old Mrs. Grannet is out of luck!"

Jab looked at me and laughed. "Now I know you joke about Mrs. Grannet wanting to marry you, but that's all a tease. Right?"

I grinned. "Could be. Keeps Andy entertained."

We sat and sipped and were quiet. I waited for him to tell me something. Share and share. He didn't, so I prodded him. I knew there was a story in him, and for some reason, I wanted to hear it.

"How about you? Ever come close to marrying?"

Jab sat still and looked down at the ground. I lit up another Marlboro and smoked most of it waiting for him to speak.

"Maybe," he started, staring out into the night which was folding in around us. "There's been some women. Some I lived with for a while, some I just dated. There is one who is special, and I've known her for years. We were together for a time, and then I left. When I returned to find her, she was gone, and I'm not sure where. Actually, I have a general idea, but not an exact address or telephone number. I think about her. I do that a lot. Not sure what to do."

I considered what he said. I heard a wistfulness in his voice that only a fellow traveler could discern, and I felt the ache he hid. I understood. I nodded.

"Any way to find out? Contact a friend of hers maybe?"

"Tried that once but her friend was less than helpful."

I shrugged. "If she means something to you, then, don't give up. Try another friend. Bother people enough and they'll give in. At least some of the time. Life is short, Jab, and you are young enough to still have what you want. If you think she's what you want, you need to try. Hey, listen to me or not. I'm just an old meddler."

Jab looked over at me and smiled. "I know you mean well, Gil."

We sat and finished the tea and talked more about things that weren't so close to the bone. I smoked the rest of the pack of Marlboros, and we decided it was time to call it a night. We put away the chairs and began to walk towards the house. Jab stopped at the stairs.

"I think I'm going to walk for a while, Gil. Not ready to sleep yet. See you in the morning."

I waved him off and went to my room where I hoped I had another pack of the cigarettes. Needed one more for tonight. Bad habit, I know. Wish I could give them up, but there's few enough pleasures in life. Gosh-dern habit. Going to be the death of me yet.

West Virginia Pepperoni Rolls

Recipe #1   **Note: will take an entire day**

Buy the ingredients, assemble all the bowls and baking equipment, measure out the exact amounts, mixing and kneading it together according to the detailed directions.

Spend all morning kneading and resting the homemade dough, but be careful not to overmix or over knead.

Wait. Clean baking equipment while waiting.

Make sure you have the correct amount of pepperoni and slice it carefully to place inside the dough which may be ready.

Place measured and prepared rolls on prepared cookie sheets and bake until brown and crusty. Watch carefully.

When ready, take out the super-hot sheets and run a stick of butter over the baked rolls and allow to cool ten minutes.

Eat. Then clean remaining baking equipment.

Recipe #2

Walk to *Jilly's* on Main Street in Wisteria, West Virginia.

Order as many rolls as you can eat.

Wash them down with a chilled Mountain Dew or two.

Sigh with contentment.

9. Watch (Broken)

I don't know whether my life has been useless and merely a misunderstanding, or whether it has a meaning.

Because TIME is (was, and will be) a man-made concept, constructed to provide some form of power over a brief existence, concocted to dictate duties and tasks imposed upon men by men, constituted into smaller portions to maintain management and manipulation, Jab never thought he needed a watch. So, as he glanced at his wrist to note the hour and minute, he turned on the equipment for the afternoon's first bowling lane customer: a father with three children, and smirked at himself, a form of self-criticism and self-reproach. And at the same time, he, once again, admired the watch.

It was early afternoon and the *Blue Waters Bowling Lanes* just opened for customers. Jab, who had worked his way from lane cleaner to bowling shoe attendant to part-time night manager and now, full-time manager, welcomed them. As manager, well, one of two, the other being the owner, Matthew Waters, thus the moniker which flashed in neon just above the large swinging doors of the structure at the northwest side of Columbus Ohio, Jab worked often and diligently. He had labored at the lanes for almost two years and was constantly questioning his life choices. He was over four decades old, wondering how long he could continue his transient lifestyle, considering his future. Two years. Too long.

Many months ago, he appeared at the office of Matthew Waters and applied for the job advertised. It was becoming winter, and through the years of traveling and wandering, Jab had always settled someplace during the winter months, ferreting out a job or two, putting down makeshift roots until spring when he would sometimes stay, often leave. He began to work at the bowling lanes as a *Lane Maintenance Attendant* from ten at night, which was when the bowling alley closed, until two in the morning. Of course, it was not just the lanes he was cleaning, but the floors, the bathrooms, and the shoe counter. After working a few nights, he noted that the shoe counter was in disarray, and, having extra time because he was diligent, Jab cleaned it, reorganizing the shoes which had not been replaced properly. Matthew Waters noticed, and when, out of anger at the current shoe attendant's noncompliance with organization and cleanliness he fired him, he offered Jab the new job. Jab took it. Then, after proving his diligence once again, he was promoted to night manager so Matthew Waters could go home and be with his wife and family, and then, a while later, Jab was made full-time manager. The entire process took six months. Jab was closing in on his second year at Blue Waters, but he had determined that when spring arrived, he would be gone. In the meanwhile, he worked, slept in the seedy hotel where he had taken up residence, continued to read, think, and reflect upon his life. And admire his watch.

The watch. It was a Vintage Citizen Automatic men's watch which could be started by the shake of the wearer's wrist. It was kept running by the movement of the wearer and had a black face and a black leather band and identified the date. A new one was not very expensive, and had Jab wanted to, he could have bought one for about forty-five dollars. The thought never occurred to him. This was a found item. One evening, as he was cleaning the men's bathroom, he discovered the watch on a sink. He put it in an envelope and placed it on Matthew Waters' desk with a note. Matthew Waters questioned him during the following payday, asking about where it was found and commenting that Jab was an "honest fellow who could have kept the item". Jab looked at him and said, "It wasn't mine", a statement which so impressed Matthew Waters that he remembered it. Honesty was in short supply at the bowling lanes. The watch was kept in the Lost and Found for months but never claimed. When Jab was promoted to the full-time manager's position, Matthew Waters gave him the watch. "Keep it. No one has come for it, and it runs and looks decent. You don't have one, so you?" he asked. Jab did not. So, he took the watch and the job, accepted the new sky-blue Polo shirt which announced his promotion and had *Blue Waters Bowling Lane*s stitched across his heart, and earned both a bit more money and the additional trust of Matthew Waters.

When Jab first arrived at the Blue Waters Bowling Lanes establishment, it was starting to turn cold. Time to settle for a while, wait out the winter, find some work and a place to plant temporary roots. He had been wandering for a few years. When he left West Virginia, Jab hadn't paid attention to the directions on the interstate highway and headed east instead of west which was what he originally intended to do. Once he realized where he was, he was almost to Pittsburg, and because it didn't matter where he was going, he continued eastward and landed in the *'Burgh*, as he discovered it was called. He stayed there for a couple months, finding, as always, a place to stay and a temporary job. Then he left. He wandered east, staying for a time in Harrisburg, Pennsylvania, then to Buffalo, New York, then back around to Akron, Ohio, and dozens of small towns along the way. He worked in stores, at restaurants, as a delivery person, in bars, and for a time, at the Columbus Zoo and Aquarium where he took the second shift as a Security Ranger. He liked that job, and enjoyed walking around at night, watching the nocturnal animals, feeling a kinship with them. He might have kept it, but because he couldn't produce the exact documents the place required, including a CPR certificate, he was let go after a couple months. Then he saw the ad for the Blue Waters Bowling Lanes, and decided to move on to a job not requiring additional schooling.

Jab liked Matthew Waters who, being about twelve years older than him and having three teenagers at home, was delighted to find someone who was older, willing, and able to take over some of his duties in the business. Matthew's wife, Connie, taught at one of the local high schools, and while she was able to assist at the lanes during the summer months, was kept busy by her own work duties and the three boys who were themselves busy with school and sports. Jab had gotten to know the entire family having been invited to their house for various holidays, and the sights and sounds of the Waters group created a longing for a stable life and a brand-new yearning for a family. The longing and yearning taunted his nomad experience, his restless essence, his rootless existence, and he vacillated between accepting his life and regretting it. Part of the issue was due to his reconnection with Meri.

Not a reconnection in the sense that Jab was seeing her or speaking with her, but he had obtained her address in Indiana and had resumed his habit of sending her periodic postcards and short notes. He sent one every couple of months, but was unsurprised when he never heard back from her. She didn't know where he was, and he never included a return address or phone number. He wasn't even sure she had received the postcards, but hoped she had. After several years of calling some of her friends and hounding them for information about her, one of them broke down. She said, "I'll give you her address, but that is it. And never call me again!" He was happy to oblige.

But lately, he began to consider seeing Meri. It had been years, and he couldn't just show up, although that was his original plan. He had taken Matthew Waters into his confidence and discussed the issue with him one late afternoon in fall when it was cold and beginning to snow, and only two lanes were open and being used. Matthew Waters and Jab leaned against the shoe counter, talking and waiting for the players to complete their games. The weather was turning bad, and the regular bowling leagues had cancelled for the night. The bowling lanes would close early. Matthew Waters took a sip of the water he held and swallowed it before he asked another question.

"So, you haven't seen this woman in ten years or so and you think she's still available?"

"Don't know. Not sure of anything. Her friends wouldn't talk to me about her, and I just don't know. The only thing I have is her address, and she has no address for me."

"Well, what do you want to do? What are you trying to find out?"

"I suppose I want to know if she wants to see me. That's a start. It means I need to let her know where I'm staying. I could send her the address at the hotel, or their phone number, but they aren't careful with messages. Remember the times you tried to contact me and couldn't?"

Matthew Waters took the last long sip and nodded his head. "Jab, give her the address and phone number here. If something comes in, I'll let you know."

"Are you sure you won't mind? No guarantee I'll ever hear from her anyway."

"Sure, do that. Something happens, I'll let you know. Are you sure she isn't married? Has kids? There could be plenty of things that happened over that many years."

"Not sure about anything. But I'll write her a short note and send it out. Thanks, Matt."

"Hey, anything for love! OK, that lane is done, and the other is close to finishing. Let's start to clean up and close. Snow's coming in hard," and the two managers started the closing prodedures.

Jab did write to Meri telling her to send any reply to the bowling alley address. He didn't hear back and wrote again. He asked if she wanted to see him, if they could talk, if it were possible to reconnect. But there was no answer. He wrote once again, after Christmas, in the new year, and decided that if he didn't hear back this time, he would have his answer. He drove to the post office to deposit the letter into the proper receptacle. After doing that, he opened it once again and peered into the darkness to ensure the letter had dropped into the pile of mail at the bottom. Not paying attention because his mind was consumed with a possible future, he let the metal lid from the letterbox go and it slammed down on his wrist, on his watch. He examined it, noting the watch was still working, but the lid had fallen on the crown of the watch, cracking it, and rendering it useless. He would no longer be able to set the time. Jab sighed, and took this as a signal from the universe that his quest was hopeless.

He didn't hear back from her. He considered sending another note, but thought he had sent enough of them. Either she hadn't received them or wasn't interested in seeing him. He assumed the problem was his fault. He should have returned to Tennessee sooner, should have tried harder, should not have been so useless, and now, where was he? What did he have? A meaningless life. A solitary existence. He hadn't even kept in touch with his own sister. He berated himself over and over, falling into despair and becoming so quiet and despondent that Matthew Waters grew worried about him. When the bowling lane mail arrived daily, he scoured through it, hoping to be able to call Jab into his office and hand him an envelope containing a reply to his entreaties. Even a negative reply from that woman would be acceptable. Then at least, Jab could continue with living, could form a new friendship, perhaps even find a new woman who would appreciate him. Connie's youngest sister, Crystal, was available, and Jab even knew her. Matthew Waters planned their pretend courtship in his head, visualizing Jab thanking him profusely on their wedding day, grateful that his new wife would make him (somewhat) part of the Waters family. Matthew Waters was a romantic at heart.

Winter waned, and spring arrived. Weeks had passed since the final note had been sent, and Jab knew he had his answer. He grew edgy with the good weather, jealous of the migratory birds he watched fly into the trees which were starting to bloom, disgruntled at the job he had held for a considerable amount of time. He was skittery and flighty and jumpy, and Matthew Waters saw this and knew why. No one had to tell him. He knew that Jab would not be around to help with the influx of summer bowlers, to facilitate with the organization of the summer leagues, to assist in the ordering of extra items for the vending machines. He could see the active agitation in this man and knew the outcome.

During a lull one afternoon, Matthew Waters approached the subject of Meri one last time. He hesitated at first, not wanting to aggravate an already aggravated situation, but decided Jab might just want to talk about it.

"No, I guess not. I suppose I have my answer, Matt," and Jab sighed.

"I don't want to pry, and you don't need to answer me, but what did you write in your last note?"

Jab looked at the floor and then up at Matthew Waters' face. "It was short. I just asked one question: *Do you want to see me again?* That was it."

The two of them stood there silently. There was nothing more to say. Jab had his answer. He knew he would leave, and he knew that Matthew Waters knew it too. He wasn't sure where he was going to journey. Perhaps to just outside Chicago, to see his sister, to talk to her and to Steve, and renew a relationship with his nephew and niece who were by now, half-grown. Maybe back out to South Dakota to visit friends, to discuss life and beliefs under the chokecherry tree. Possibly voyage someplace strange, somewhere new. There was a spirit in him that was unstable, unpredictable, uncertain, and he had to follow its dictates. Travel. Wander.

***

A week later, Matthew Waters walked out to the mailbox to gather the daily mail of bills and advertisements. He grabbed the handful of envelopes and went back to his office. Jab was due in anytime now. There were new leagues forming, and he needed to speak with him about them. He knew that Jab would be leaving soon. Nothing had been said, but hints had been dropped. Matthew Waters put the pile of mail on his desk and thought he needed some coffee. He poured himself a cup, took a sip, and sat down in his chair. Jab came in and stopped in the office to greet him. They spoke for a few minutes, and then Jab left to complete his daily routine. He was just about finished when he heard the intercom. It was Matthew Waters' voice.

"JAB, PLEASE COME TO THE OFFICE IMMEDIATELY. JAB, PLEASE SEE ME RIGHT NOW!!"

Afraid of what had happened, Jab thought back to the time some kids had opened the front doors and shoved two stray dogs in, or the incident where an older woman had fainted, or the birthday cake fight that had erupted between two groups of teens, and he hurried back to the office where Matthew Waters was standing at his desk waving an envelope at him.

"It's for you!"

Jab caught his breath and took the envelope. He examined the return address, one with which he was familiar, and took an additional deep breath in an attempt to get enough oxygen. Neither of the men spoke as he nervously tore open the envelope and expectantly removed a single sheet of paper. Time, as noted on Jab's found, and now broken watch, as created by man, as monitored by his heartbeat which could be heard throughout the universe, stood still, as the single sheet was opened.

Matthew Waters waited and watched. Jab looked up at him and his expression was unreadable. Mathew's romantic heart beat with suspenseful possibility, and he itched to know. "Jab," he demanded, "What did she say?"

Jab turned the single sheet around so that his friend could see what was on it. As Matthew viewed it, a smile filled his face causing his cheeks to balloon. There, in large letters was a single word. It contained the answer to the repeatedly asked question. It was the solution to where Jab was headed next. It was the response to Jab's self-agonizing wondering about his life: was it useless or meaningful? On the sheet was the reply for which Jab had been waiting:

Yes!

Matthew Waters

I was delighted for Jab when he got the answer he waited for. He was ecstatic. I don't think I had ever seen him smile like that, and that entire day, he practically floated on the air. He was usually a great worker, but I couldn't fault him for not doing his usual upstanding job because his mind was somewhere else. Somewhere in Indiana, and I was glad for him. And sad for me. I really liked the guy. It's not often you meet someone so honest and hardworking. I think Jab could have done anything he wanted to, been anything he desired, but there was that part of him that needed to move, to travel. We talked about it often enough, and I didn't have an answer for why he was like that. He didn't either.

Not me. Born here in Columbus, Ohio, met Connie in high school, went to Ohio State University together, and while I couldn't hack it, Connie could and did. We married in her senior year, and we worked and saved, and bought a small house that, over the years, has been expanded. When the opportunity came up to own the bowling lanes where I had worked as a teen, we borrowed from both our parents, took out a big loan, and here we are. The boys came along, and now the oldest is a high school senior and planning to go to Ohio State next year. Good thing he's smart and got a scholarship. Hope the other two get some help although I'm not so sure about the youngest. He may be taking over my job. In the meanwhile, Jab is leaving, and I'll need to look for a replacement. That will be difficult.

Jab and I have spent plenty of time together talking and learning about each other. At first, I thought he might be interested in dating Connie's younger sister, Crystal. I talked to Connie about fixing them up, and was surprised she wasn't for it.

"Matt, I love my sister, and Jab seems like a good enough person, but really, how much do you know about him? Crystal has gone through boyfriend after boyfriend, and even though she's almost thirty, I just don't see her settling down. Let it alone. Jab is here enough times and so is Crystal. If something were to come of that, it should be their decision. Remember when you tried matching Crystal up with the bowling shoe salesman? What a mess. Let them be. Honestly, I think that if they were interested in each other, something would have happened by now."

She was right. I believe in the Noah's Ark two-by-two plan for life, and I have made a few mistakes with my romantic fix-ups. I tried to match Connie's unmarried friends up a few times, and Crystal more than once, and I'm apparently not good at it. I think myself a romantic, and claim that as the reason I wanted Jab and Crystal to get together, but if I'm to be honest, the thought of Jab in the family, working at the lanes and helping me out for a lifetime, sends delicious chills down my back. Down my selfish back. Connie's right.

I didn't ask Jab about when he was leaving, but I knew he would before long. I thought I should just wait and let him come to me. It took about three days before he showed up in my office as I was finishing paperwork. It was his day off, so I knew that if he were here, it would be to hand in his notice. I looked up from my desk and he was standing there holding a white bag from Buckeye Doughnuts, a place we both loved. He smiled and put the bag down. Then he went to the coffee maker and put on a fresh pot. I finished the sheet I had in my hand then pushed stuff to the side. Jab poured and fixed two cups of the hot coffee, pulled up a chair, and sat down on the other side of the desk. I opened the bag, took out the chocolate cake doughnut with the chocolate frosting I knew would be there, and took a bite. We sat and ate and sipped and finally, I spoke.

"You're leaving. Right?"

"Yes, Matt. You know where I'm going and why. I wanted to sit and talk to you and thank you for taking me in and giving me a job with decent pay. I appreciate all the home-cooked meals from Connie and really liked being around your boys. I'll miss all of you and will try to stay in touch. But I'm not good at that, and I want you to know it. I can't thank you enough for your help."

I wiped my hands on the paper napkin and took a long swallow of the coffee. "It's been a pleasure getting to know you, Jab, but you should go and see what the deal is with Meri. I'm curious. Why didn't you call her? You could have found out her telephone number. You had her address. You could have asked her some of the questions you want to know. What if she is married? Have you thought about that?"

"Thought plenty about it. I want to keep some hope, so I didn't want to know too much too soon. Something tells me that she isn't married, that she's available. In fact, I think she's waiting for me. That sounds strange, but sometimes, I just know things. And I have a feeling about this."

I took another doughnut. "Hope you're right. And if she's married? What then?"

"Then I'll accept that I really messed up, wish her well, shake her husband's hand, and leave. Go see my sister and her family. Go out west again. Go somewhere different, some place I haven't been. Travel. Done that all my life. I can continue it."

There was nothing to say to that except, "So, when will you leave?"

"In about two weeks. I'll finish out this week and do another, and help you with the summer stuff as much as I can. I know you'll need to get someone to take my place, so you should probably advertise the position."

"I know. I will. And I'll get the summer schedules and vending machine papers to you by tomorrow. Did you call the repair guy about those two lanes that aren't working right? We need to fix them before the leagues start."

"I fixed them," said Jab.

"You did? Great! Honestly Jab, I'm going to miss you and for more than just your ability to fix about anything. How about coming to the house Sunday? I'll put up a sign and close the place early. You can see Connie and the kids, and I can get the grill going. A proper good-bye."

"Sure. Sounds great. Now, since I'm here, let me do a quick check of things. Be back in a bit," and he got up to work. On his day off.

I watched him go and make his rounds. I walked out and checked the two lanes which were not working. They were fine. Jab had repaired them, saving me money. *That guy can do anything,* I thought. And then: *Anything except stay in one place.* I'm going to miss him.

10. Magnet:
There's No Place Like Home

Even the hour of our death may send
Us speeding on to fresh and newer spaces,
And life may summon us to newer races.
So be it, heart: bid farewell without end.

"That one," said Jab to Meri as he simultaneously pointed to something and scooted under the motorcycle, an old ragged towel underneath his back to protect his shirt, "…the one over there." Meri picked up the screwdriver and handed it to Jab.

"Thanks," he said, and continued to work at repairing and correcting and adjusting the motorcycle which had been moved to the middle of Meri's garage. Her car was out on the driveway; the garage door was open allowing sunlight to flood the area; Meri was seated in a lawn chair watching while Jab continued to work; Meri's daughter, Ellen, was next door playing with her friend. It was an early Sunday afternoon.

The motorcycle had been in the garage for three years and needed major restoration. The battery and fuel lines needed replacing as did the seals and gaskets; the chains needed lubrication; even though it had been stored correctly and the tires were off the ground, they had turned brittle. New ones were needed. The Triumph Thunderbird had been purchased by John, Meri's father, who kept it in unblemished condition even after his riding days were over. He would start it and let it run, polish and clean it, and work on it as long as he was able. After his death three years prior, it remained covered in the corner of the garage, a reliable, high-quality machine, waiting for a new owner to claim and refurbish it, waiting for Jab.

"So, your father rode?" Jab asked Meri when he first examined the bike.

"When he was younger. My stepmother didn't want him to have one because she was afraid of them. After she died and I moved here with Ellen, he decided to buy one. He didn't ride much, but was happy playing around with it, sometimes riding for a bit on nice days. He wanted to take Ellen with him, but she was too small, and I didn't think it was safe. Having the bike made him content and kept him busy. He loved spending time out here polishing and cleaning it. Ellen would stay out here with her toys and keep him company. It was Dad's hobby. When he died, I didn't want to get rid of it. I just couldn't. What do you think? Is it repairable? I'm serious about you having it. I know you liked to ride."

Jab checked around the bike, noting what was needed to get it going again. "I haven't had one for years. That old truck of mine isn't going to last much longer. I've babied it, and it runs good, but I wouldn't mind selling it and getting another bike. This one's not bad, Meri. Let's find out what it's worth, and I'll buy it from you."

Meri shrugged. "You can have it, Jab. Really, it's just here taking up room, and I know Dad would be glad that someone will care for it. It's yours."

Jab shook his head. "No. I said I'll buy it from you. It needs some major repairs, but I can do them. It'll be good to work on a bike again. I'll find out a fair price for this."

"Well, I'll tell you what," and Meri grinned, "I remember losing a bet to you once, for ten dollars. Pay back that ten, and the bike is yours."

Jab grinned back at her. "I still have that same ten dollars. Never spent it. Won't give it back, but I have a new bill I can offer you."

"You still have it? I would have thought it would have been spent long ago."

"No," said Jab, "not that one. Do we have a deal?' and he stuck out his hand.

"Sure," laughed Meri, and when she took his hand and shook it, he held on to it. She held his hand too.

Jab checked around for a fair price and paid Meri. On weekends and some weeknights when he wasn't working at the restaurant, he would arrive at Meri's and tinker with the bike for an hour or two. Ellen would come in to the garage and watch him, asking questions about the tools, listening to him explain what he was doing. She was friendly and inquisitive, and Jab, who was not used to children, discovered he enjoyed having her around. At times, he would look closely at the girl and wonder, but nothing had been said to him, and when he broached the topic of Ellen's parentage, Meri's answers were vague and circumspect. After one such questioning, she told Jab that she didn't want to talk about it, and he stopped asking. Besides, it was really none of his business. Jab didn't want to forfeit their restored friendship or his current status in Middletown, Indiana.

When he left Columbus to travel to Middletown, he wondered about what would happen, what he would say, what Meri would say, what she would be like. He drove around the small town, looking for the house on Blackberry Street, considering what to do. Should he just march up to the front door? Perhaps he should have brought a gift, but what? What was Meri's marital status? It was never mentioned. If she is currently married, will her husband object to a friendship with a former boyfriend? He hoped she wasn't married. As these thoughts ran through his mind, he found Blackberry Street and the house which was on the corner across from a small park. He pulled his truck to the park side, turned it off, and sat staring at the house. The attached garage door was open and in it was a car. He rolled the truck window down and watched the house, waiting, feeling both nervous and impatient. A young girl turned the corner and steered her bicycle into the garage. She came out bouncing a ball up and down the front walk for a time before flipping it back into the garage. Then she walked up the stairs, opened the front screen door and went in. Who was this? Meri never mentioned any children. But then, she never wrote much, just that he was welcomed to visit, and she wanted to see him. He glanced at his wrist, forgetting the watch no longer worked and was stored at the bottom of his duffel bag. He needed to do something, so he got out of his truck.

He shut the truck door, leaning against it, summoning up courage to walk towards the house. As he waited, a familiar woman exited and walked down the stairs to the mailbox at the bottom. She reached into it and gathered the mail, standing for a minute to glance through it. As Meri started to walk up the stairs, she turned and looked over her shoulder, glimpsed Jab, and stood still. They stared, statues by a park, and then began to walk towards each other. Meri waited at the curb as Jab stepped up. She smiled.

"Hello, Jab. I was wondering when you'd get here. Are you coming in?"

Jab, uncertain as to whether a jealous husband was watching from behind the front drapes, did not do want he wanted: he did not reach out and gather Meri into his arms. Instead, he replied, "Sure, Meri. I'd like to do that."

There was no jealous husband, just a young daughter, Ellen. Jab stayed for dinner and learned the rudiments of Meri's life as they sat and talked, and when it was getting late and Meri offered him the extra bedroom, Jab lied and told her he had taken a room at the motel he had passed. He would stay there until he decided what to do, and Meri didn't question it. They parted, this time with a hug, and an invitation for dinner the following night. Jab traveled back to the motel and did get a room. This was the start of a tentatively sowed friendship; one which had lain fallow for a decade.

He stayed at the motel for a week while making decisions. He found a job. He rented a room, cheaper than the motel, at a small boarding house, and he and Meri and Ellen began to spend their weekends and free nights together, grilling out in Meri's backyard, walking in the park just across the street, going for ice cream during the warm summer nights. When the motorcycle business came up, Jab spent even more time at Meri's house, working on the bike, and eventually, at Meri's suggestion, a suggestion which he welcomed, he moved into the extra bedroom. At least that was the official story.

The three of them formed a unit. Not a family unit, but a domestic circle of sorts. They adjusted to each other's schedules, and when late summer came and the fall school session began for Ellen, they readjusted, making next-day lunches at night, testing Ellen on her weekly spelling words for Friday's test, spending weekends, when Jab didn't work, at festivals and country fairs, riding to the events in Meri's car which Jab tuned up, saving Meri the trip and cost of a repair shop. Jab was introduced to the neighbors and to Meri's friends as her *long-time companion and friend,* and was accepted as such, although unasked questions remained. Meri and Ellen modified and amended their duality and included Jab, becoming a trinity. Jab was more content than he had been for years. In what he considered his dotage, he contemplated settling down, meditated over the outcome of staying put, ruminated upon putting aside his wandering, pondered about living in Middletown, Indiana with Meri and Ellen, her daughter. He watched the young girl and wondered. Thoughts resided in his mind, but he kept them to himself, kept them shrouded. He waited and watched.

A fall festival was to be held on the fairgrounds in Elkhart, just thirty minutes away, and the three of them planned to attend. Jab switched his work hours from Saturday to Sunday, and before they left at noon on the appointed day, he checked Meri's car, filling the gas tank, and running it through the car wash. He drove it back, spent an hour

with his motorcycle, took a shower, and sat in the kitchen, waiting for
Meri and Ellen to ready themselves for the trip. Once they were set and
the house was locked, they got into the car and drove west along US-20,
finding the fairgrounds where they parked and got in line at the gates.
Ellen removed her sweatshirt and tied it around her waist expecting
the warmth of the noon-sky to continue. A walk around the fairgrounds
was the first order of business. They examined the rides and games
and booths and exhibits, and made plans to revisit those which were
of special interest. Ellen ran over to a booth touting posters, magnets,
wooden signs all marked with quotes and catchphrases. She pointed to
some of them and laughed at their familiarity and humor in a way that
only a ten-year-old knows.

"Look, Mom, *Eat My Shorts* is my favorite saying. It's soooo
funny! Bart Simpson is great! Can I get the poster for my room?"

Meri looked at the poster and made a face. "Let's see what else
there is. If you get it now, you'll need to carry it around the entire time
we are here. We'll be back this way and can always pick it up before we
leave." Meri was trying to avoid the maternal *No* she felt bubbling up in
her throat, so she took what she thought was the neutral way out.

Ellen sighed and shrugged and continued to look around. Poking
at the magnets which were on the spinning spindle stand, she asked, "Jab,
do you see anything you like?"

Jab stood next to her looking through the sayings. "Some of
these are funny, I guess." He stopped and looked at one flowery magnet
whose red block letters pronounced *There's no place like home!* He lifted
it off the stand and looked at it. His sister's face flashed in his mind, and
he remembered Jan smiling and saying those words. Ellen glanced at
the magnets, spun the stand around, and moved next to her mother who
was looking at some dried flower arrangements. Jab continued to hold
the magnet. He took it to the older woman seated next to a cash box
and paid for the item, shaking his head when asked if a bag was needed
and slipped the magnet into his jeans pocket. He wasn't sure why he
even bought it. Perhaps one day he'd see Jan and bring it to her. They'd
laugh as he placed it on the refrigerator, and she'd hug him. Jab was
smiling as he rejoined Meri and Ellen. He remained in a contented mood
through the remainder of the day, and when they left the fair after hours
of viewing and laughing and eating, they stopped back at the booth with
the posters. Jab bought the Bart Simpson poster for Ellen who hugged
him while Meri resignedly shrugged, then smiled. That night, Jab helped
Ellen attach it to the wall of her bedroom. Then he put the magnet into

the bottom of his duffle bag next to a pack of playing cards and some green-colored pens.

Life for the three continued and became some sort of normal. Holidays for Jab were no longer something to be ignored. Traditions were dredged up from his memory and honored. Halloween and Thanksgiving and Christmas and New Year's Eve and Valentine's Day and all the minor instances in between were marked, were recognized. Jab took part in the decorating and the parties and shopped for the special foods and gifts. It was a remembrance of childhood and a past life, and brought with it guilty sensibilities about his own ignored family: his sister and her husband and their children. They roamed through his mind, ghostly presences, rambling, meandering, appearing at unexpected moments. When Ellen dressed up in her Halloween costume, Jab remembered taking his five-year old sister from door to door, collecting unnecessary cloying treats which Jan lovingly shared with him. When the neighbors joined them for Thanksgiving, bringing a creamed corn casserole which was so exactly like the one his mother used to make, he took a bite and looked around the crowded table, ready to compliment her, momentarily forgetting she was gone. After helping to adorn Meri's house with the red and green and glittery white trappings of the holiday season, he stood back and thought about the times he and his father had traveled to the local florist to purchase a real tree to bring home and decorate. And when Meri arrived home on a snowy night, secret gifts and packages filling her arms, she plopped down in a chair and sighed, "There's no place like home!", Jab felt a lurching in his stomach and knew he would travel to that suburb just outside Chicago in the new year. He needed to see his family. He wanted to be with them and explain to his sister that he was ready to end his vagabond life.

The trip would not happen during the winter months. Jab had decided to ride his newly refurbished motorcycle, and the Midwest weather was not conducive to riding. Besides, he was enjoying the times he and Ellen were able to play some of her favorite board games. Sometimes Meri would join in, but usually she just watched as they threw the dice or moved their markers or straightened out their cards. Spring came and went, and Jab was busy working in the yard of Meri's house where he planned to plant a small garden. He thought some tomatoes and green beans and onions would do well and was anxious to plant and weed and harvest with Ellen who showed an interest in eating those vegetables.

The early summer came and went, and the weather, which was lovely, encouraged Jab and Meri and Ellen to walk across the street and enjoy the park area where they sometimes brought snacks or sandwiches with them. Meri watched while Jab and Ellen played catch with the baseball and mitts Jab found in the garage. Then summer was almost over, and Jab knew it was time. He hadn't said anything to Meri yet. One late evening, when Ellen was asleep and the two of them were in the back yard enjoying the sometimes breeze and watching the stars, Jab knew it was time to announce his plans.

At first Meri was quiet. Then she asked, "Will you be coming back?"

Jab reached for her hand and held it. "Yes, I will. I haven't spoken to my sister in years, and I need to. The guilt is building up, and I want to spend some time there, getting to know her and the family again, and try to explain myself. I'll be gone for a month or so, but I'll be in touch, and I'll be back. I want the two of you to meet. You'd like her. We are a decade apart in age, but we've always been able to talk. Jan just accepts me and my choices. I think the two of you will get along. In fact, I know you will. Her husband, Steve, is a stand-up guy, and the kids, at least what I remember of them, are great. Older than Ellen, but they'll get along too."

Meri rubbed Jab's hand. "Jab, when you return, there's some things we need to talk about."

Jab looked up at the stars and they were quiet for a time. Then he said, "Yes, I know," and for the remainder of the time they were outside that evening, nothing else was said.

There were only a couple weeks left in the summer. Meri and Ellen planned a Saturday shopping trip to search for clothes and shoes for the upcoming school year. Later that day, when Jab came home, he asked Meri how the shopping went.

"We found some things, but everything is so expensive, and I just couldn't afford the kind of shoes Ellen wanted, so she's pouting. She went next door to play with her friend, and I told her to make sure she was home for supper. Think we'll make burgers on the grill tonight. Maybe that will perk her up."

Jab looked at Meri and started to say something but didn't. He reached over and hugged her and said, "Sorry it wasn't a success, and I'll do the burgers. Let me take a shower and change," and he went into the bedroom. He reached into the closet where he had some things stored.

Before he took a shower, he examined his duffle bag, pulling items out and rearranging them. Then he cleaned up and went to help Meri.

The burgers were useful in lifting Ellen's spirits, and after the food was put away and the dishes cleaned up, Jab asked Ellen if she wanted to go for a walk.

"Is Mom going?"

Jab shook his head. "No, just the two of us. Let's go to the park and walk around it. Meri, we'll be back in a bit," and they left.

As they wandered around the small park, watching some of the neighborhood children using the swings and slides, Jab spoke to Ellen.

"Ellen, I'm going to leave for a while next week. My sister and her family live near Chicago, and I haven't seen them in years, so I'm planning to visit for a time. I just wanted you to know."

Ellen kicked at a stone, and then bent down to pick up another one. She examined it and threw it into the dirt before she said anything. "Are you coming back?"

"Yes, I am. But I want to spend some time with my family. And while I'm gone, would you look after the vegetable garden? You know what to do."

They continued to walk on the path which serpentined around the grassy area. Ellen looked sideways at Jab. "OK, Jab. I can do that. What's your family like?"

Jab told her about Jan and Steve and his nephew, Jim, and niece, Kate. At least what he remembered. He answered Ellen's questions and when they came around to their starting point, they crossed the street and went into the house where Jab removed some ice cream bars from the freezer. The three of them sat in the back yard, eating the bars, and talking about nothing important. They simply sat and talked and joked, and when it was time for Ellen to go to bed, she hugged her mother, shoe disappointment forgotten, and then hugged Jab, something she hadn't done often. Not since the Bart Simpson poster had been obtained. She went to bed, and Jab and Meri continued to sit outside.

"I told her I was leaving for a time," said Jab. "She was fine with it and asked questions about my family. She's a great kid, Meri, and you've done a good job with her."

Meri looked down at the grass and then sighed. "Jab…" she began.

He stopped her. "Wait, Meri. Let's talk later, when I return. Let's not start a big conversation before I leave. OK?"

Meri agreed. "Alright,"

"However," began Jab, "I need to get a few things ready for my trip. I need some paper and a couple envelopes. Also, there are some things in the bottom of my duffle bad which rattle around. Do you have a bag I can store them in? That way they'll stay in one place."

"Sure. Do you want them now?"

"That would be great. While you are tucking in Ellen, I'll settle those things."

They went into the house where Meri found the paper and envelopes. She handed them to Jab and then handed him a couple small paper bags. Meri grinned as she held up a cloth bag, the kind someone would purchase at a souvenir shop to give as a gift. There was a nature scene on the front with flowers and some bees and a cursive saying which read: *What a Wonderful Day!*

"How about this one?" she asked. "Not sure where I even got it, but it should do for holding a few things."

Jab laughed. "Perfect," he said, "I'll use it," and he took the items.

Meri went to the back of the house to be with Ellen, and Jab went into the bedroom where his duffle bag was waiting. He took a small envelope, placed an exact amount of cash into it and wrote *Jan* in the front. Then he placed it into the hidden zippered side pocket of the bag. He wrote and placed a brief letter into the second envelope along with additional items and put that into his duffle bag for later delivery. He took the paper bags, tearing them into sections and wrapped items from the bottom of the bag. Then he carefully put them: drumsticks, a folded ten-dollar bill, a Swiss army knife, three pens banded together, a beaded keychain, a woman's scarf, a pack of playing cards, a broken watch, an old Polaroid photo in a plastic baggie, and a refrigerator magnet, into the cloth bag decorated with flowers and bees. He folded the bag and placed it at the bottom of the duffle bag next to a blue-covered book. The duffle bag was placed back into the closet where it would be ready for a trip the following week.

***

Tuesday morning was a cloudy day. Jab was ready to leave. He waited until Tuesday because that was Meri's day to go into work late. Ellen was still sleeping, having stayed up late the previous night, playing card games with Jab and watching an old movie with him and her mother. Jab carried her to bed when she fell asleep on the couch, and after he pulled the light coverlet over her, he leaned down and gently kissed her forehead. He stood for a minute and then went back to Meri. Together they turned off the lights, locked up, and went into the bedroom they shared.

The following morning, Meri was in the kitchen preparing to cook. "Don't you want breakfast?" asked Meri. "I'll make those pancakes you like. You should eat before you leave."

Jab finished the glass of water he was drinking and shook his head. "Thanks, but I want to get started before too many trucks are on the road. Hope it clears up today because I'm not thrilled about riding in the rain. If it rains, I'll stop and grab a bite, but I'm not hungry now. Listen, Ellen knows I'm leaving, but she didn't know it was today. I don't want her to be upset when she finds me gone."

"Let me wake her up," said Meri. "She'll want to see you."

"No, let her sleep. I know she'll go to her friend's house when you go to work, and you can tell her then. She was so tired last night," and Jab smiled at recollection.

He finished the water. Meri looked at him. She was determined not to cry. She didn't want to upset Jab and felt she didn't have a right to demand anything from him. The past year had been a good one, and she had been happy. She was sure he had been happy too. Without saying anything, Jab picked up his duffle bag and looked at Meri. They walked out to the garage.

He moved the motorcycle to the driveway and checked it once again although he was sure it was in perfect condition having worked on it for months. It was reliable and smooth-riding, and he was looking forward to getting out on the road again. He was anxious to see his family after such a lengthy hiatus. He was sad to be leaving Meri and Ellen and reluctant to prolong the good-byes. He attached the duffle bag to the back of his seat, tugging at it to ensure firmness. Jab turned back to Meri, walked towards her, and gathered her into his arms, holding her as she let out the sob she was attempting to stifle.

"Don't," he said into her ear while he kissed her face, "Listen to me: I'll be back. And when I return, there are things we need to talk about, things neither of us are saying, but I know, Meri. I know."

Meri did not ask what he knew. She understood. She was having a difficult time stopping the tears and felt angry at herself for crying when she had prepared herself, steeled herself, determined not to allow her sadness to spoil their farewell.

Jab held her and said into her ear, "I left something for you on the dresser."

He felt Meri nodding. She whispered, "I just can't say *good-bye*, Jab. This is difficult for me."

Jab nodded back. "Difficult for me too, Meri." He kept her close and then looked at her. He kissed her and smiled. "In the Lakota language, there is no word for *good-bye*. The closest the language comes is *toksa akhe*. That translates to *later, again.*" He kissed her once again and whispered, "Toksa akhe, Meri. Later, again."

They held each other for a time. There were no more words. There was no need. Jab let her go and walked to the bike. Before pulling on his helmet, he turned to Meri, giving her a significant, sad smile. He swung his leg over the bike, started the vehicle, and sat on the seat for a few seconds. Without turning around again, he steered steadily out of the garage and onto the street which separated the house from the park. Mistiness ruled the morning. Fog dropped down around him as he rode away. Meri stood for a long time, watching Jab disappear into the murkiness, hidden by the hazy blur. She gazed into the milky morning until she couldn't see him or hear any noise, then turned and walked heavily into the house.

Letter to Meri

Meri,

Three things.

First: the money in this envelope
is for you and Ellen. There's $3200 in it.
Use it for Ellen's needs. Get her those
shoes she wants and for her school clothes or
fees or anything else that is needed. Think about
putting some of it in a bank account for a college
fund. She's a bright kid and has a future.

Second: I know.

When I return, you and I need to talk and make a plan
for our future. We need to sit down with Ellen and let
her know who I really am.

Third: This past year has been the happiest of my life.
You are the one.

        J.

IV.

The
Burial

*My life, I resolved, ought to be
a perpetual transcending,
a progression from stage to stage...*

The Burial

i.

It took me a while, but I finished the book. I'm not sure what I was supposed to understand about it or about Jab's interest in it or how it influenced his life and beliefs, but I didn't understand any of those things. The book was engaging and complicated, and philosophical in a way I couldn't grasp. There were parts I found completely incomprehensible, and other parts I reread for the flowery flow of the language. But I read it, and I will attempt, at some point in the future, to reread it. I believe it's one of those novels whose meaning and importance can only be appreciated upon studying it. I don't think my mind has the abstract metaphysical bent Jab's did. Or at least I think his did. Anyway, when I finished it, I placed the blue-covered book on the top closet shelf next to Jab.

Jab. I would periodically pull out his duffle bag and examine the items again. One night, after Steve and I finished a bottle of wine, and both the kids were out with friends, I said to Steve, "Come on up to the bedroom. I have something to show you." He was apparently expecting something other than the display of items in the duffle bag, and I laughed at his obvious disappointment.

"You didn't tell me you even received the box," he commented. "Why not?"

"I'm not sure," I answered, "I wanted to see what was in it, and examine it by myself. I've been thinking about this for a while now. I needed to consider what it all means, and I want your opinion. Look at these things. Why did Jab keep them? It's not as if they are valuable, although they must have been to him. He wrapped some of them to keep them safe. What do you think?"

Steve picked up one item and then another. He examined the photograph and turned it over and over. All the things were laid out on the bed, and he went from one to another, moving them around, shifting one and then another, trying to match things up. Finally, he shrugged and looked up at me.

"I don't know, Jan. You're right. These aren't worth anything, and I can't figure it out. It's a puzzle with no solution. What are you going to do with them? Keep them? Throw them away?"

"No," I said, "I can't throw these away. They meant something to Jab, and I need to honor that somehow. I don't know what to do with them."

"What about Jab? How long are you going to keep his ashes in your closet? Jan, your brother needs a proper burial. Do you want to think about that? I can investigate some things for you. We should consider what to do."

"I suppose," I answered, and the two of us rewrapped the items, placed them back into their cloth bag, then into the leather duffle bag. They were returned to the back of my closet.

****

ii.

Steve did his research. My parents and his father were buried at the same cemetery, so one day, without telling me, he visited the business office and came back with information for me.

"There are *columbaria* or cremation niches available for Jab's ashes," he explained. "I asked if they might be large enough to hold other items beside the urn, and there are various sizes, so if you want to, Jab's treasures can be buried with him. A plaque can be engraved with his name and a saying or something, if you want to do that. There is always the option of burial in the ground. I checked, and there is a space close to your parents for Jab. You can decide."

I thought about it. "No, not in the ground, and not next to our parents. I think Jab would prefer to be by himself. Don't you? Thanks, Steve. We should do this for Jab. Our family can have a small ceremony for him."

"The columbaria are outside in a wall, and there are some benches placed around them, so if you wanted to visit him you could. Why don't I make an appointment for us? We'll go there, and you can see for yourself if that's what you want to do."

He did that. We went. It was the right thing to do for Jab.

***

iii.

A short time later, right before Jim would go to college and Kate would begin her junior year, the four of us went to the cemetery and held our own short ceremony for Jab. The Memorial Service Director, Mr. Phillips, was understanding, and I appreciated his compassionate suggestions. He led us to the wall and stood back as we held our brief remembrance. I had *The Glass Bead Game* with me and had marked some of the quotes to read. I didn't expect to cry, and didn't expect either Jim or Kate to, but we all did. Even Steve's eyes clouded. The plaque was not yet ready, and Mr. Phillips said he would call when it was in place, and I could come out and examine it. After we left Jab, we visited my parents and then Steve's father, and then, trying to put death behind us, we went out to lunch. It was a simple burial, befitting Jab, suitable and proper for a brother I barely knew.

At the restaurant, I told any stories about my brother I could remember. I recounted the times he visited, and encouraged Jim and Kate to talk about what they remembered. Kate didn't remember much, but Jim did. He talked about the toy horse Jab had sent him, and how it was named *Tadita* after the one Jab said he would ride. After a few stories, they both began to remember the toys and gifts that Jab sent to them years ago. I explained about the items that had been buried with Jab, and Jim asked about the duffle bag.

"Do you still have it? Is it in good shape? If you don't want it, it would be cool to take it to college with me. Can I?"

"Sure. It's in decent shape for being so old, but leather lasts. Let me clean it up. I'll put it in your room for you to look at, and if you still want it, then keep it," and we finished our lunch and went home.

That evening, as Steve and Jim watched a ball game on television and Kate stayed in her bedroom talking to a friend on the phone, I went upstairs and got the empty duffle bag from my closet. Although it was leather and in good shape, I would make sure it was useable and decided to wipe the outside with a special solution and clean the inside before giving it to Jim. I took it downstairs and went out to the patio to shake out any stray dirt. I opened it up and reached inside to gather the lining when I felt a zipper. There was a small zippered pocket hidden on the inside, and I felt something there. My heart began to beat rapidly. What if this was an address book, or a diary, or more photographs? Could Jab have placed the answers to his secret life in this pocket? I unzipped it and removed an envelope. On the front of the envelope, in Jab's flowing handwriting was my name: *Jan.* I sat down on the nearby chair and carefully opened the sealed envelope and reached inside. I pulled out, carefully organized by denomination, cash. Money. I knew how much it was before I began to count it. It was two hundred dollars.

I sat there with the cash in my hand. I thought about the magnet with *There's No Place Like Home* embossed on it, the one buried in Jab's columbarium with him. Jab was coming from South Bend, Indiana, and according to the police report we received, was headed west when the accident occurred. West. Towards the Chicago suburb where we lived. I don't know why he was in South Bend, and maybe he wasn't. Maybe he was simply traveling through, but every fiber in my being, every atom in my body told me he was headed here. Home. He was coming home.

There was no way to prove this; there was simply my feeling. In a day or so, as I lay in bed with Steve and explained my theory, my assumption, he would agree with me. I don't know if Jab would have stayed, but that opportunity was gone. I would never know. I glanced at the cash I clutched, and I knew he was coming here to return it. Two hundred dollars. *Just a loan*, he wrote in that last note he left. I counted the cash once more and considered it. I would give one hundred dollars to Jim and the other hundred to Kate and tell them it was from their uncle. Their Uncle Jab.

I sat on the chair and cried. I allowed myself to grieve, to mourn, to lament, to feel anguish for the brother who taught me to play chess and ride a bike, who gave me a bracelet for my twelfth birthday, one I still had, who sent the carefully woven baskets which still decorated the hallway, and gifted me the silver dragonfly necklace I wore daily. I ached for the brother I never knew and the moments we never shared. Anger and sorrow mixed together in my tears. Anger at Jab for leaving and for returning and for leaving again. Sorrow for never allowing me to know about his life. I was angry at myself too. I was selfish in not insisting he stay, in being so ineffective in convincing him, stupid in my own heedless, egotistical, and self-absorbed actions. I sat and cried. Then I stopped.

I wiped my face with the bottom of my blouse and stood up. Placing the envelope into my jeans pocket, I took the duffle bag, shook it out, and felt around the inside to satisfy myself that it was completely empty this time. Then I thoroughly examined it once again. I sat down, placing the old leather duffle bag next to me. Tomorrow I would use the leather cleaner on it before putting it in Jim's room. Tomorrow I would give Jim and Kate the money from their uncle. Tomorrow I would tell Steve about Jab's probable homecoming. But tonight, this night, I would sit outside by myself, watch the darkness, face and accept my anger, my sadness, and think of dragonflies.

***

iv.

A couple weeks later, Mr. Phillips from the cemetery called to tell me that the plaque for Jab was completed and in place, and I was welcomed to view it any time. On an early fall Saturday, I took a solitary trip to the cemetery. Steve was working on a backyard garden project; Kate was at work, waiting tables at a small diner; and Jim, well, Jim was at college. I hoped he was studying, but I knew the weather was too inviting for that to probably be the case. I went out to the yard to tell Steve where I was going and left.

I maneuvered the car through the large open gates of the cemetery and drove slowly along the wide lanes until I got to the columbaria where I parked the car close to the grass so it would not be in the way of other cars. The area was empty and quiet as I walked over to the free-standing wall and found the niche where Jab and his treasures had been settled. I examined the plaque and smiled. It was perfect. I ran my fingers over the letters and read them out loud:

1947-2000
Jonathan Alexander Boyd
Jab
Son, Brother, Uncle,
Seeker

There was a bench directly in front of the wall, and I sat there and thought of nothing. I allowed my mind to wander, to not worry or ache or think of anything. I just sat on the bench with my brother. *What a Wonderful Day!*

In the quiet of the afternoon, I heard a sound. I turned to watch a car slow down and park directly behind mine. A young woman, maybe a few years older than Jim, got out and walked over to the wall. She gave me a friendly look, a shy smile, and then walked to the wall and stopped at the niche next to Jab's. She stood there and did what I had just done: she ran her hands over the words of the niche. Then she lifted her fingers to her lips, kissed them, and placed the kiss on the plaque. She stood for a minute and then turned to me and spoke.

"These were my grandparents. Whenever I'm home for a visit, I come here to see them. They were wonderful people, and I miss them."

I nodded my head and said, "That's a thoughtful, loving thing to do; a sweet way to remember them."

She smiled. "I like coming here. It's calming. There are unusual stones around, and I read some of the names and dates and wonder about the people buried here. I wonder about their lives, who they were, and what they did." She glanced at the wall to the left and then the right. She turned to Jab's niche and examined it. Then she read it out aloud: "Son, Brother, Uncle, Seeker."

She ran her hands across the letters of the last word. S-E-E-K-E-R. "Seeker," she said. She turned and smiled at me and spoke, "I hope he found what he was seeking."

I looked at her and then at Jab and remembered the items which rested next to him in the bag decorated with the flowers and bees. I thought of the blue-covered book which was in my bedroom on the nightstand because I was rereading it. I considered his final journey and remained convinced he was coming home. Coming home to see me and Steve and Jim and Kate. Coming home to talk to me, to tell me about his life, to explain the significance of the items he kept safe in the duffle bag, perhaps even to stay. Coming home. I wondered at the complexities of life, the conundrums, the mysteries, the dilemmas, all the absurdities, the paradoxes and complications. The stillness and warmth of the afternoon brought ease as I sat on the bench. I took a deep breath, smiled back at the young woman and confessed, "I hope he did too."

V.

Kapemni

V. Kapemni

The man walked out of the light which was so bright it burned. But there was no pain in this place. There was no hurt or sorrow. He stepped onto the stars beneath his feet and thought I want a bench, and one appeared. He sat on it. He waited and watched. Many people came: men, women, children. The children ran right in. They were not stopped. At times an adult was sent back out and began to walk and within a dozen steps, disappeared from sight. But the man sat on the bench and looked to the distance. Time did not pass. There was no time in this place, no morning or night, no hours, no ticking clock. The man saw the being for whom he waited and watched. He stood as the second man came closer.

They met face to face. The first man smiled. He waited for the second man to speak.

"Where am I? I recognize this place. I have been here before."

"You have," said the first man, "but you were sent away. Now you may enter. Come. We will enter together."

The two men walked to the start of the stars which burned but did not pain. The brightness was blazing and dazzling and gleaming, but it was also soothing and reassuring and tender. The men walked.

The second man stopped to look around. He turned to speak in this place where there were no noises, no words, no voices, but the first man heard.

"I know you. We sat under a chokecherry tree once. We talked. Is there such a tree here?"

The first man nodded. "If you want there to be. Look," and he pointed, "There is a tree," and one appeared in this place where no plants lived. "We can sit and talk."

"We sat under the tree on chairs. Are there chairs?"

"Look," said the first man, "There they are," and they approached the chairs in this place where no possessions were needed. They sat down.

The second man looked closely at the first one. "You are familiar. You spoke to me and told me tales. I listened. I don't remember it all. Will you explain it to me?"

Takoda smiled and nodded. "Yes, my brother. I will."

Against the lustrous luminosity, the blazing brilliance, the intense incandescence, in this place where no sound was necessary and no words were significant, he spoke.

Recommended Reading

The Glass Bead Game by Hermann Hesse

(Also published as *Magister Ludi*)

Except where otherwise noted, all quotes are from Hesse's

The Glass Bead Game.

In 1946, Hesse was awarded the *Nobel Prize for Literature*

for the book, his final novel.

Coming next:

Susan M. Szurek's new novel:

A Thousand Fibers

In *Tomas' Children*, Mrs. Ingrid Vogel was introduced.

A Thousand Fibers

is her story.

An excerpt from the novel follows.

Excerpt From   *A Thousand Fibers*

One

Bonneville, Illinois

1922

"Maybe you should just stay out of her business," replied Mr. Anderson as he used his cane to maneuver himself up from the wooden kitchen chair, the one he had repaired years ago. "Anyway, I need to get going. The horse and wagon are there, and I'll be at the side of the house when he's ready to leave. Let him know I'm waiting for him."

His wife nodded and handed him the brown-paper wrapped package that had been given to her. "Remember, she said to wait until you drop him off to hand it to him. And as far as her condition is concerned, I *can* help her, you know. She doesn't have to have it, and I know she is early enough along so that it won't be a hard loss. She hasn't said anything to me, but will once he's gone. And good riddance. Once you leave with him, I'll check those herbs in my case. I expect she'll come done here soon. You better go. I hear him on the stairs."

Mr. Anderson left, holding the package in one hand while using the cane with his other. Mrs. Anderson shut the door behind him and went into the kitchen to deliver the message and make the offer of a breakfast. Today the man wouldn't be eating in the dining room with the lady of the house. She suspected he wouldn't eat at all but would just leave. She was right. After drinking a cup of coffee, he went back up the stairs to pack his things. The woman watched him leave, then walked into the three-room suite she and her husband shared, pulled out the small leather suitcase from under their bed, and began to mull over what was inside.

***

As Ingrid stood behind the curtain, she saw Thomas turn around to stare at the second-floor bedroom window thinking she was there. She knew he would look and was sure he wouldn't think to lift his eyes up one floor, to the third-floor, to the servant's quarters, to connect with her eyes. She watched until the wagon driven by Mr. Anderson turned onto the road to town, and the blooming early spring tree branches hid them from her sight.

She stood for a minute longer, and then, feeling faint, sat down in the corner chair. She took deep breaths and willed the morning sickness away. It worked. At least for a time. She would go back to her bedroom, the one on the second-floor, the large, ornately decorated one she had shared with her husband. The one attached to the dressing room which housed the smaller bed, the one in which, years ago, her husband, Fredrick Vogel, died. She would lay down in her bed and sleep a while. Mrs. Anderson had been told to leave her alone until she came downstairs, and she would. She knew Mrs. Anderson suspected. She always knew the secrets.

Ingrid took another breath and rose from the chair. As she passed the other servant's bedroom, the larger one, she saw Thomas had removed the bedding, folded it, and left it at the foot of the bed. The sun pressed into the room and lit up the small mirror over the washstand, drawing her attention to it. She noticed something on the stand and walked over to see what it was. Thomas' comb which held a few of his dark hairs had been left. She touched his hairs, brushing her fingers gently against them, but did not remove them. Turning, she departed the third-floor bedroom while cradling the comb in her hand and went down one flight of stairs to her bedroom. Walking to the ornate dresser, she opened the top drawer where she kept her jewelry, and placed the comb next to the velvet-covered box containing a special gold and emerald bracelet. She shut the drawer, turned, and went to her bed where she lay down trying to make herself comfortable. She would rest for a time. Then she would find Mrs. Anderson and confide to her the secret she presumed was already known.

Two

Ingrid Winthrop

Despite her grandmother's conscientious ministrations: the academic dictates, the designed tutoring in music and etiquette and languages (both French and German), the conservative but fashionable clothing, the appropriate age-specific books, toys, and games, the necessary introduction to society and friends, the careful choice of an expensive, elite boarding school, Ingrid was aware of her grandmother's dislike of her. Perhaps not when she was so young, when she was just a couple years old and her parents' horrific deaths placed her into the care of Louisa Winthrop, her paternal grandmother, but certainly as she aged, as she noted the punctilious tone of derision when her grandmother spoke to her, the deliberate stares she was given when Grandmother Louisa didn't realize she was being seen, the lack of physical contact which her friends and their parents often shared. There were enough of these instances that Ingrid, at twelve years old, feeling a bit grown, sought to question the reason for the dislike.

She was home for the summer, having returned from the spring term at boarding school. She and her grandmother were seated at the dining table eating a late summer supper when dessert, always fresh fruit in season, never a sweet which was saved for special holidays or a birthday, was served. Ingrid watched her grandmother take a careful bite of the peeled and poached peach placed with care in the everyday blue and white china before she spoke.

"Grandmother, can I ask you something?"

"*May* I ask," Grandmother Louisa corrected. "What is it?"

"Why don't you like me?"

Grandmother Louisa stopped mid-chew and swallowed before placing her spoon down and her hands in the lap folds of her dove-gray dress, the mourning color she had insisted upon wearing years beyond the social expectation of the tradition. She looked at her granddaughter, surprised at the question, shocked at the directness.

"Nonsense, Ingrid. I do love you."

"Not *love*," and Ingrid looked back into her grandmother's eyes, searching for the truth. "I asked about you *liking* me."

Louisa Winthrop hesitated just a moment, almost allowing the sorrow at her only son's death and the dislike of his dead wife who was this girl's mother show through her narrowed eyes and twisted mouth and clutched hands. But she held herself and took in a shallow breath and drew the curtains across her visage, arresting any show of emotion. She picked up her spoon and raised another small piece of the peach to her mouth, wondering if she would be able to move it down her closed throat.

"What silliness you bring up. I love and like you the appropriate amount. Such a question! Now, finish your dessert and then go practice the piano before you get ready for bed."

Louisa replaced the uneaten spoonful, pushed the dish away, and nodded to the standing servant. "Have Cook seep some peppermint tea," she ordered. "My stomach needs a soothing agent." She was soothing the wrong organ. It was her heart that had broken at the death of her son, her only child. It was that organ which wanted soothing, which craved healing, which was past peppermint protection.

***

The last decade of the nineteenth century held multiple sorrows for Louisa (nee Barnard) Winthrop, wife of George Winthrop of the esteemed East Coast Winthrop family. The New York winters were dreadful, and the usual plans were being made for moving to the Winter Colony in Aiken, South Carolina where both George and Louisa would enjoy the comforts of the resort and the splendor of the sun until the snow in the northeast was mostly melted. Their plan was to depart immediately after the usual Christmas Day celebration. But the snow came earlier than expected that year. In early December, as George was returning from a late evening at his club, he and his carriage were caught in an intensely severe and unexpected ice storm. It was late when he left his carriage stuck in the muddied and iced streets, instructing his driver to disengage it, a task which would take some hours. He determined to walk home to his large house which was only four streets down from the Vanderbilt mansion on 57th Street. He arrived cold and soaked and stayed in his wet evening dress while he warmed up with a brandy. But the chill turned to a cold and then a fever, and a mighty, hacking cough took residence in his chest, and plans to travel south were abandoned. For a month, doctors were seen coming and going from the tall brownstone, all of them expressing various opinions and producing an assortment of tonics and tinctures, none of which helped. Christmas at the Winthrop estate that year was a quiet and solemn affair, lacking joy and good will. By the second week in January, a few remote relatives and friends had made the journey to visit George Winthrop a last time, commiserate with his wife, and wipe counterfeit tears decorously, using expensively detailed Irish linen handkerchiefs.

Meticulous funeral traditions and constancies were observed throughout the following weeks and months. George Winthrop was dressed in his newest suit and settled on his bed with a decorated and hidden cooling board beneath him and massive (in both size and expense) floral arrangements surrounding him. This allowed for closest family and intimate friends to say their farewells comfortably. Mourning clothes were ordered and rapidly created, and Louisa's long black public veil was readied. Black crepe was tied to the front door's bell knob as reminder to visitors of the sorrow inside, and black lined notecards and stationery were ordered for required personal correspondence. Eight members of George's club received letters on the black-lined stationery requesting them to act as pallbearers, and all except the one who remained at the Winter Colony in Aiken replied they were honored to assist. Another friend was found. The obituary published in the *New York Times* was, as expected, only a few lines, and the indication of a "private funeral" was understood. Death required traditional specificity, adherence to exactness, and unstated bounty, and no one would have been more cognizant of that than George Winthrop.

In 1877, when Cornelius Vanderbilt died, he was buried in the family plot at the Moravian Cemetery in Staten Island. Because George Winthrop, although he did not know the man personally, admired his wealth, he purchased his own family plots there in 1880 and arranged to be buried as close to the Vanderbilts as possible. Unfortunately for the Winthrops, Cornelius and his family were reburied in 1888 in what became known as the new Vanderbilt Mausoleum in the Vanderbilt Cemetery adjacent to Moravian Cemetery. But plots had been obtained, monument stones had been readied, and the original cemetery purchase became George's final resting place. Louisa Winthrop realized that the distance to the cemetery and the winter weather would necessitate the small procession to travel for a lengthy time. The carriage ride would take close to two hours. Multiple carriages, needed to transport the immediate family, necessary relatives, the minister, pallbearers, and a few friends, were hired. This task was supervised by George's son, Von George Winthrop. Afterwards, a quiet but splendid dinner would be offered to the mourners who would be exhausted after the consuming day and were due refreshment. That too required planning and organizing. Louisa had hoped to be assisted in this task by Von's wife, but the woman, Eliza, claimed her delicate condition precluded her from both the planning and the long cold journey to the cemetery. While Eliza refused kindly and spoke logically to her mother-in-law, and although Louise understood and capitulated to the woman's decision, it did not endear the younger to her elder. It added to the unhappiness that the widow felt. Even when the baby was safely born in early April of 1889, the event provided additional chagrin and sorrow for the grandmother. The child was, unfortunately, female.

***

www.ingramcontent.com/pod-product-compliance
Lightning Source LLC
Chambersburg PA
CBHW061305210726
48293CB00003B/1118